The Sleepless

The Earlyworks Press High Fantasy Challenge

The Sleepless Sands

The Earlyworks Press High Fantasy Challenge

This anthology, title and cover design copyright © 2006 Kay Green. Cover Illustration © 2006 Katy J Jones. Cover design and title based on 'The Binding of the Sleepless Sands' © R D Gardner 2006. Copyrights to all stories and illustrations remain with their individual creators.

All rights reserved. No part of this publication may be reproduced, stored in a retrieval system, rebound or transmitted in any form or for any purpose without the prior written permission of the author and publisher. This book is sold subject to the condition that it shall not be lent, resold, hired out or otherwise circulated without the publisher's prior consent in any form or binding other than that in which it is published.

ISBN 0-95534429-3-7
(ISBN from Jan 07: 978-9553429-3-6)

Printed in Latvia by

DARDEDZE HOLOGRĀFIJA

Published by Earlyworks Press
Creative Media Centre
45 Robertson St, Hastings
Sussex, TN34 1HL

www.earlyworkspress.co.uk

For more of cover artist Katy Jones' work, visit
www.katyjones.co.uk

Introduction

Any story which is woven with imaginary characters or settings can be called **fantasy**. It saves the writer hours of research say the cynics - no need to check facts - as long as the facts are true to each other within the story you can break any rules you like. One of C R Krishnan's apparently traditional Indian tales has a god whizzing around in a helicopter! That's fantasy, but not high fantasy. If you like it, you call it a festival of imagination. If you don't, you call it pointless escapism. By contrast, **high fantasy** has rules. It must be true to myth, to the nature of men, women, beasts and, well, nature. The dragon (and his cousin, Dracula) *will* lust after virgin blood. Even if they join a cold turkey club (see Terry Pratchett) the lust is still there. We all know it's in their nature. Leprechauns will give wishes but their gold will not outlast the dawn. Selling your soul to the devil will not have a happy ending...

I give this definition because the loosening of the rules in recent years has devalued the genre in many people's eyes. To my mind, high fantasy must have what Tolkien called 'applicability' i.e., you can use your own instinctive knowledge of life and culture to test the story, and you can use the story's weaving to test yourself. It must be applicable – but not simple **allegory**. Animal Farm is both fantasy and allegory, but isn't high fantasy. **Magic realism** is fantasy, but not high fantasy. The fantastic has a guest appearance in magic realism, but doesn't drive the plot. **Science fiction** is fantasy, but not high fantasy because it is made up of predictions for the empirical world, not dippings into the mythic or psychological one.

Many readers and critics think the range of high fantasy is limited and it's dying out as a result. I believe this is only true to the extent that the range of the human mind is limited. It depends on the imagination and ambition of the individual, whether reader or writer. And that's why we set the challenge as follows:

"Please, no more magic sword romps," they say. "Elves, dwarves and rustic spirits have had their day. High fantasy has scraped the barrel clean, there is no more."
To win this competition, prove them wrong! Send us a new fantasy story or poem that feels as magical as one of the old favourites, but isn't just a rehash.

This book celebrates the work of those who we feel answered the challenge with heroic success.

The overall winner was R D Gardner for "The Binding of the Sleepless Sands". We chose this story to start the collection for a number of reasons: The elements of the story are traditional, and true to their mythic form; the story is well-crafted and original; the plot is excruciatingly applicable to the political, social and psychological dilemmas we face today. When I first read it I loved it but felt uneasy about the unresolved issues it left. When I passed it to Katy for illustration she felt 'traumatised by the fate of the butterfly boy'. A quick look at the daily papers will explain both these reactions!
The poetry prize dangled for some time between R D Gardner and Steve Mann. Gardner's "Wizardry and Second-Hand Romance" is a clear demonstration of our problem – why some people think high fantasy has outstayed its welcome! – But Steve Mann's "…and here he is, himself…" gives us the solution: We see the modern seeker tentatively approaching our mythic hero, and coming back with something new. And Mann's "Kismet" closes the collection on a note all high fantasy should end with – doubt, paradox and possibility. The range of poems, stories and artwork in between is enormous. Traditional, modern, comic, romantic and deadly – but every one adds something to the cauldron. Enjoy them and take heart – the sun is not yet setting on high fantasy!

Kay Green, August 2006

Contents

Stories		Page
The Binding of the Sleepless Sands	- R D Gardner	1
Last-Cloud-of-the-Rains and the Fire of the Gods	- R D Gardner	7
Peredur and the Crystal Cup	- Caroline Clark	20
Silver Stream	- Caroline Clark	40
The Good Knight and the Castle of the Bears	- Douglas Bruton	43
I Have a Daughter	- Catherine Edmunds	59
Gandeel	- Sue Hoffmann	75
Little Teeth	- Jenny Black	97
The Doom of Mournshire	- Benjamin Sperduto	106
The Path Less Travelled	- Charlotte Bond	125
Why the Stars are the Way they Are	- Felicity Bloomfield	149
The Hurl and the Stone Rose	- Perry Mc Daid	152
Which Way is Heaven?	- Natasha Monroe	160

Poetry   **Page**

Wizardry and Second-Hand Romance
                                              - R D Gardner   12

Word Weaver II: The Rock of Silence
                                              - Helen Francis   14

Yellow Leaves   - Anne Murphy   15

...and here he is, himself...   - Steve Mann   18

Unicorn   - Derek Adams   34

Did You Hear the Sword Sing   - Derek Adams   35

Dreams, Visions, Reflections of the Lady of Shalott
                                             - Sally Richards   36

Oh To Be Silver   - Dee Gordon   38

Victorian Cadence   - Carly Dugmore   147

Kismet   - Steve Mann   168

Artwork

Cover and details: 'The Sleepless Sands' by Katy J Jones after 'The Binding of the Sleepless Sands' By R D Gardner

In text:

Knight by Nikola Temkov	13
Dragon Slayer by Nikola Temkov	58
Comic by Jenna Whyte	105
Elemental Telecommunications by Suryan Philip	148
Diamond Throne by Suryan Philip	151

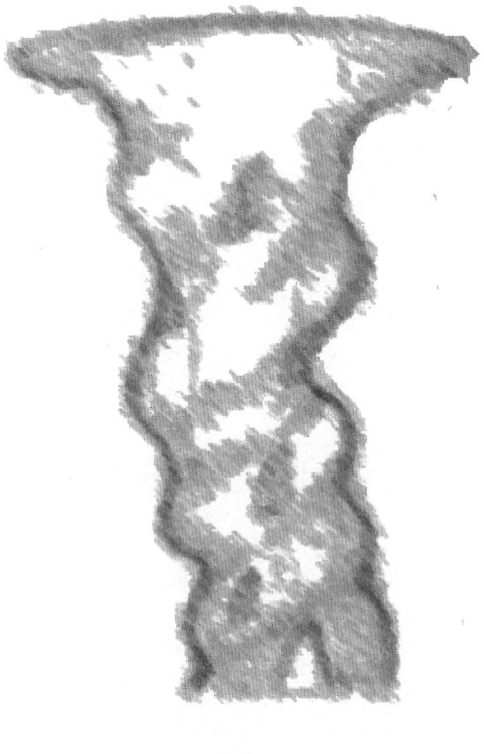

The Binding of the Sleepless Sands

by R D Gardner

A new moon rising over the southern border of Phemerae, and a wizard without a shadow was strengthening the spells that held back the Sleepless Sands. He worked by the light of a single candle, whose steady flame burned bluer than the moonlight that sharpened the edges of the dunes. The tower on whose top the wizard stood looked something like a candlestick itself, twisted in a spiral and flaring wide at the top. An architect would have noticed how the spirals grew broader as they rose to the tower's flat crown; he might also have noticed the crushed mortar and misshapen windows, and speculated about the origin of the tower's name: the Dragon Tower.

Tonight, however, the Dragon Tower less resembled a candlestick than a lighthouse in a rising storm. The curved front of an immense grey dune reared above it like a wave about to break; another dune pressed up behind that, and another, as though a gale out of the south were chasing them down on the tower – and certainly, they had not been there yesterday, nor before sunset had there been a single dune within bowshot of the Dragon Tower. Such little wind as there was blew from the west, but the waves of grey sand came marching up from the south before the driving malice of the desert lands, to break on the defences of the Empire, or to overwhelm them.

Before the terrible weight of that wave stood the wizard, and at his side was a boy who had walked out of the living lands at sunrise, with the scars of shackles on his wrists and a swarm of white butterflies tangled in his long black hair. He had stood before the tower like a sleepwalker not yet wholly awake, while the butterflies lifted strands of his hair to the dawn wind.

The wizard, who never went outside in daylight, allowed the door to open for the boy, and soon heard his weary, uncertain tread on the stone stairs that wound around the tower, worn smooth, sloping and irregular like shelves of rock over which the sea has long washed: heard him pause, more than once, at the places where the sprung stonework bulged inwards. A bright lad, then.

"Welcome to the Dragon Tower, my son. Come in, take some wine with me – you have travelled a long way."

The boy took a hesitant step over the threshold, staring timidly about him in the shimmering light of colourless glass lamps suspended from the ceiling like a flight of freshly-blown bubbles. The wizard's room had no windows: they were shut away behind the metal panels which coated the walls in a seamless sheet of milky silver. They reflected nothing, but threw back the light from all sides and in all directions, so that nothing in that room seemed to cast a shadow.

"You called me…in my sleep."

"I did," the wizard smiled. "I searched for you, and called you, and then I sent the butterflies to bring you – but they have done their work now."

He brushed the butterflies casually from the boy's hair. Under his hand, they changed into white cyclamen blossoms, which fell to the floor and withered at once.

"What is your name, my son, and how old are you?"

"Yeaver. Fifteen."

"Hmm. Yeaver, son of Nobody? Yeaver, the Runaway Slave? – Yes, I see you have worn chains. Well, Yeaver of Nowhere, if you live through this night's work, you will be Yeaver the Wizard, Yeaver of the Dragon Tower: a worthy career for a young man, no?"

Yeaver sank into the chair that the wizard indicated, looking more bewildered than ever. The wizard poured pale, fragrant wine into glasses like the ghosts of lilies, flicking the trailing sleeves of his white robes deftly out of the way. Yeaver drank abstractedly, fingering the intricate fretwork of the chair arm – and spilled wine all over himself as he realised that it was not made of fine-crafted white wood, but of carved and fitted bones.

"Bones are very strong," said the wizard reproachfully, "and take fine carving far better than wood…and if a long-dead horse can unsettle you so, I doubt your fitness for the task ahead of us. Still, the butterflies chose you, and I must not forget that all this is very strange to you. Never mind your clothes, they were unsuitable in any case. I have others for you."

He made no gesture, but a chest of bleached sandalwood opened its lid, exhaling a faint perfume. Obediently, Yeaver exchanged his frayed, wine-sodden tunic for the white robes within, of silk so fine that his fingertips rasped on it like cats' tongues.

"They fit? Good, I thought I judged your size correctly. Yes, I had them made for you: it is not difficult, simply a matter of feeding certain substances to the spiders...oh, for Meiunoth's sake, boy, are you a wizard's apprentice or a senator's granddaughter?"

Dressed in the whispering, almost weightless robes, sluicing dust from his face and arms in a silver basin, Yeaver finally found his tongue.

"I'm very pleased to be your apprentice, my lord wizard – but who are you, please, and why did you bring me here? And what am I going to have to do tonight? And...and why do you live in a silver box, like a sugared almond?"

The wizard smiled, and poured more wine.

"You will call me Master, naturally, but when they remember me in the living lands they call me Ward, the Wizard of Light. Only light can drive out the dark, boy, and I live in this silver box because I will have no darkness about me, and no shadows. For where there are shadows, there is doubt, and where there is doubt, there will be confusion, and where there is confusion, there will be *Chaos!*"

The wine glasses jumped and rang as his fist crashed on the table.

"And that we cannot allow, my boy," he continued, with a kindly smile at the speechless Yeaver, "for if I were to fail in my duty tonight, the sands that devoured the cities of Imataria, and sent the proud Imatari forth as hunters in the wilderness, no longer remembering that they ever built with stone – those sands would be gnawing on the walls of Imperial Thesiaeas itself before the Emperor had cracked his breakfast egg. And so we come to the most vital of your questions. Tonight is the last new moon of the old year, and the bindings on the Sleepless Sands must be renewed, in the teeth of that power which stirs the desert like the sand-clock of Chaos. I have held back the desert for three hundred years, and I am growing old. I need a young man's strength beside me, and steadier hands than mine on the Dragon Staff – and I need a successor. There is a night of fear ahead of us, but if you see tomorrow's dawn, all my secrets will be open to you, and you shall hold the Dragon Tower when I am gone."

So it was that a slave-boy from dusty Peralepida, where water is so scarce that ornamental fountains display glittering jets of blown glass, stood on the Dragon Tower at moonrise, watching his solitary shadow flicker on the cracked flagstones. His white robes swirled like steam in the night breeze; his black hair was bound by a circlet of sliver, blade-thin from centuries of polishing, bearing a baroque pearl in the shape of a human heart. The staff rigidly gripped in his scarred hands seemed restless in the blue-edged candlelight: a grey steel shaft, twined about by a sinuous, limbless dragon of red gold. The dragon's half-opened wings flared above the staff, which was crowned by its reared head, jaws threateningly parted. Beside Yeaver stood the old wizard, his white head bare. The rod in Ward's left hand was of plain ivory, without even the mystic runes which Yeaver would have considered essential to a wizard's staff, in his right hand was a sword of cloudscale steel, its shimmering blue splashed with patches of shadow etched by a dragon's blood.

It was the dragon killed by that marred sword that Ward and his apprentice were summoning. The broken strings of sibilants, scarcely resembling language, that made up the wizard's incantation echoed around their heads as though he chanted in a cave, seeming to reverberate not only from the looming slope before them, but from invisible angles within the air itself. At intervals, he made a slight gesture with the ivory rod, and Yeaver, raising the Dragon Staff imperiously, recited one of the sequences of phrases in which Ward had drilled him during the day. At first he felt sick and remote with fear, a puny manikin piping nonsense syllables beneath the monstrous crushing power of the Sleepless Sands, but as his responses chimed out and nothing stirred but little scurrying dust-devils, confidence built to exhilaration. He brandished the cold, heavy image like the standard of Light, and the air thickened, shimmered, swirled in a lazier motion than the seething sand below. A golden glimmer coiled about the tower; wings insubstantial as heat-haze mantled above Yeaver's head, but the Wizard of Light never faltered as the dragon-shape coalesced. A rap of the ivory rod on the stones recalled Yeaver to his duty; he raised the staff that chained the dragon's spirit though the desert blanketed its bones, and spoke the closing words of the spell with all the conviction he could muster. The tower creaked like an old man's back as the dragon gained in substance, but it remained a creature of gilded glass, glittering but transparent, jaws open in what seemed a soundless laugh. It clapped its diaphanous wings; the candle flame guttered wildly, but there was no sound other than the rushing and hissing, reminiscent of a cold wind in long, dry grass, as the sand dunes began to pour themselves forward.

"On your knees, *now!*" the wizard snapped.

Yeaver fell to his knees, and as he bowed his head, the cloudscale sword struck one vicious, precise blow. The Dragon Staff lay in Yeaver's spilling blood, and the silver circlet rolled free with the sound of a ringing glass.

The dragon's laughter because audible; a noise between the roar of a forge-fire and the reverberation of a struck gong. It twined about the tower, gleaming like gold poured smoking from the furnace, and the stone blocks groaned under its weight.

"Still slaughtering your apprentices, wizard who casts no shadow?"

"I had no choice! The sands..."

"The sands are beyond your control, and have been ever since you stripped away your shadow to spite the darkness, and found your grip failing on the Dragon Staff. There is no darkness in you, Wizard of Light, and your power over Chaos is gone."

"I can still command you!"

The dragon snapped at him with blinding speed, the siege-engine jaws crashing together barely an arm's length from his head. It grinned like a wolfhound, tongue lolling over its teeth, as the wizard leapt backwards and snatched up the bloody staff.

"So I see," it observed, delicately lapping a little of Yeaver's blood from the flagstones. "With heart's blood staining that ugly staff, you still command me, but the staff grows heavy, wizard, does it not? Innocent blood weighs it down, and next year another young man will die, and then another, and the light, forsworn, dies within you, and you are growing old."

"I am defending the empire! If I can bind the Sleepless Sands no other way then I will violate my oath and pour out blood! And at last I will find an apprentice who will not kneel, and that night there will be a new wizard on the Dragon Tower...but we have a task tonight, you and I, and I will not yet be judged by those I have slain, not even you."

Light flared from the Dragon Staff, showing sand spilling down the faces of the advancing dunes to the very foot of the tower. The dragon uncoiled like a flicked whip, and the dunes crumbled under the beating of its wings. The Wizard of Light and the dragon he had killed rode a storm of fire and air and magic in the night, sang the same song, compelled the same blaze, focussed the same searing power each through the other, until the desert lay flat and submissive as a wolfskin rug under the new moon and the light of single candle, and ashes settled like white butterflies on the body of a young man from the living lands beyond.

Last-Cloud-of-the-Rains and the Fire of the Gods

by R D Gardner

In that time we lived in the trees, and used our hands for nothing more than picking ripe fruit, stealing birds' eggs, and swinging through the branches. We had long, striped tails in that time, which flew out behind us as we leaped from one tree to the next, and big, round eyes to see in the dark, because the nights were always dark before the gods came.

Wherever the gods were, there was fire. With smoke and thunder their chariots rolled across the earth, with the searing bolt of the lightning they struck, and where they struck the trees fell, and never rose again. Day and night, the air muttered with the soft speech of flames in a hearth, and smoke hung heavy about the battlefields of the gods. Then came the gentler gods, those who called new life from the earth, and the gods of things made with hands: stone palaces rose among gardens without end, and the fires burned lower. While we shivered among the windy branches, their palaces flashed and glittered, white and green and red and blue, as the night sky glitters now with the fires of their citadels above the clouds. The wild grass never set root in the gardens of the gods: every tree was heavy with sweet fruit, and plants strange and succulent sprang up where the wheels of their chariots had passed. The People of the Trees raided those gardens, as they spread further into the forest. In the first light of morning, we slipped from the branches to fill our mouths with the food of the gods, and ever and again the gods would catch us: then the air would ring with the wildness of our laughter and the thunder of the angry gods. Even as we fled, one or two would be struck down, and the hides of the People of the Trees were displayed in the market places of the gods, but still we robbed them, for the fruits of the gods' gardens grew ever larger and sweeter and more beautiful to see, and those who tasted them could be content with nothing else. The food of the gods made our hearts wiser and our hands nimbler, and loosened our tongues, so that we who had called like beasts and birds now learned to speak, but their fire the gods kept to themselves.

7

Among us in that time was a youth known as Last-Cloud-of-the-Rains, because he ran as though driven by a storm-wind to catch up with something already over the horizon. He led the most daring raids on the gardens of the gods, but always his heart turned to their fires. When the sun sank, and the low-hanging clouds reflected the high torches that lit the roads to the gods' palaces, so that all the sky smouldered orange, Last-Cloud-of-the-Rains slipped through the shadows on the edges of those roads, to climb the stone pillars, slender as the trunks of young trees, on whose crowns the torches burned, but the fire was still beyond his reach, sealed away behind ice which no blow could shatter and neither the sun's heat nor the divine fire itself could melt. He ran after their chariots when they passed in the night, but got nothing more from them than the taste of their smoke, and returned coughing and empty-handed, to the derision of the People of the Trees.

There came a time when the gods grew troubled. Often they had fought among themselves, for the gods are no less quarrelsome than we, but now they were warred upon by forces yet more powerful, and hostile to everything that turned to the sun. The clouds that hung above their citadels grew heavier and darker, until the night was brighter than the day, for the torches of the gods outshone the sun at noon: only at dawn and sunset did the sun flare out between the edge of the earth and the black pelt that was the sky, to remind us that it – and we – still lived. The wild plants sickened first: the leaves that fell did not return, and even our slight weight snapped blackened branches as we journeyed through the trees. Birds still nested in the empty treetops, but few eggs came for us to steal, and often, when we broke them open, we wished we had not. Not even the eaters of carrion throve in the deepening twilight. Although they had never fed so well, their litters became scarcer: few of their young survived, and those that died were so strange that their own kind refused their carcasses.

For a while, the divine gardens still flourished, and even seemed to grow stronger in the heavy, sunless air and the foul-smelling rain that left yellow stains on the white fur of our long, striped tails. Hunger now drove many creatures towards the gardens, but such as escaped the gods' vigilance sickened of the stolen fruit and died. Only the People of the Trees were swift and clever enough to steal from the gods and live, and the fruit we had eaten for generations did us no harm. But the blighting rain fell ceaselessly, and as the stinking, many-coloured puddles deepened into swampy pools about their roots, even the plants the gods cherished began to fail.

Then it was that the gods fled. Every night, fewer lights burned in their high windows, every day, the clamour of their works grew less, fewer voices rang in song or in wrath between the cold walls of empty palaces, and the chariots that rushed along their roads like autumn gales did not return. At last, we left the forest entirely, and lived among the orchards we had so often raided, for the gods tended their decaying gardens no longer. The search for wholesome food drew us ever closer to their walls and lightless towers, and we saw that they abandoned not only their palaces, but the earth itself. The gods in their chariots and their servants who went miserably on foot travelled always in one direction, where fires greater than any we had ever seen roared into the sky, trailing like the shimmering tails of bright birds behind chariots that flew. The filthy clouds drew aside as they passed; they vanished from our sight, and not one of them remained.

Last-Cloud-of-the-Rains, no longer a youth, but the father of many children, still ranged further among the withering trees than any of his kind, and ran more quickly than a hawk can strike. He had never ceased to dream of fire, and he grew reckless as he saw it escaping him. He climbed the very walls of the gods' palaces in search of some small, brightly burning thing to carry away, but even as he plucked a glowing torch from wall or roof it died in his hand, never to kindle again. When the last lights in the high palaces went out, and the streets of black stone were silent but for the fall of his quick, light feet among the raindrops, he swore in desperation to follow the gods beyond the hills, to rob them one last time before the clouds closed behind them for ever. The People of the Trees laughed among the dripping branches and his mate, White-Flowers-in-Darkness, refused to say farewell to him, but his two eldest sons would not let him dare the gods alone. Under clouds and under shadows they followed the gods' road to the hills, now running on the flat, cold stone itself, now taking to the trees to avoid the corpses of the gods' servants, dropped like mounds of decaying fruit rinds at the side of the road. Twice, as they travelled, a brilliant light rose into the sky: the thunder of the gods' chariot shook bitter black dust out of the branches where Last-Cloud-of-the-Rains crouched with his two sons, and when it had passed he urged them to make more haste, dreading that he would never see the fire of the gods again.

At last, they climbed a rocky hill, and saw before them a great, flat plain, where a single winged chariot rested, silver as a fish in sunlight and vast as a palace tower. All across that plain, gods and their servants fought each other, some to win possession of the chariot, some to hold it. The gods fought with thunder and lightning, so that their opponents fell like leaves from a tree when a gale rips at the branches, their servants fought as the People of the Trees fought, with sticks and stones and hands and teeth, but a god who went down under their onslaught rarely gained his feet again. When the plain was strewn with bodies, as though a flood had rolled them all down from the hills like stones, the victors did not stay to celebrate, but leapt into the chariot and gathered their smoke and thunder about them. Then, with a cry of bitter despair, Last-Cloud-of-the-Rains sprang out from among the rocks with a dead branch in his hand, he ran down to the plain as even he had never run in his life. Faster than the whirring wings of the humming-bird he ran, and the fire of the gods came boiling up to meet him, huge and bright as a sunset cloud. His sons were brave men in the fight and in the hunt, but they hid their eyes as they cowered among the rocks on the hilltop, feeling the heat stir their fur like a summer wind. The rocks themselves trembled as the last chariot of the gods rose from the earth. Shadows closed over the smouldering corpses on the plain, but one small, bright light beat them back. Last-Cloud-of-the-Rains was running still, with the blazing branch in his hand.

It was many days before Last-Cloud-of-the-Rains and his two sons returned to the People of the Trees, and White-Flowers-in-Darkness did not know her mate when she saw him again: the fire had left him neither fur nor tail, and his wide round eyes would never again see anything but the strongest light of the sun, but he brought the fire of the gods with him. That night, we lit our own fires in the gods' abandoned orchards, and we have never let them go out: truly, this fire that warms us here is the very same that Last-Cloud-of-the-Rains stole. We fed the fires through all the long nights and sunless days, when only evil-tasting mushrooms grew on the trees that rotted in the black water, and even if we starved we fed the fires still, until the sun rose again over the land that the gods had left. No longer do we have soft, grey fur and long, striped tails: our children come into the world in the warmth of the fires, naked and tailless as Last-Cloud-of-the-Rains went all the days of his life. Nor do we have large round eyes to see in the dark, we who can drive the dark before us wherever we go. The gods have settled in new palaces beyond the clouds, and the distant lights sparkle in their lofty towers. Sometimes we see their chariots trailing fiery streaks across the sky, but not one of them has ever returned to this world. We would not wish them to return, for we who are descended from Last-Cloud-of-the–Rains are no longer the People of the Trees, but the Heirs of the Gods, with fire in our hands and light in our eyes, and now this world is ours.

Wizardry and Second-Hand Romance

There is a land that only men with white-winged ships may find,
Who sail beyond the Utmost West and leave their sense behind.
There King-Professor Tolkien sits, chained to a gilded throne,
And shakes above his sycophants a rod of hollow bone
While those who pledge allegiance to the high heroic style,
But don't know half a league from half a legionary mile,
Weighed down by rune-graved cutlery advance to make their bow,
And, meaning formal reverence, address their king as 'thou'.

There, girls in brazen brassieres, with longbows on their backs,
Ride unicorns by starlight and communicate with cats.
There, noble nomad tribesmen with bright spears and manly ways,
Who, sleeping in the saddle, ride non-stop for twenty days,
Stand staunch against the Empire of the decadent decayed,
Preserving ancient legends of the Banner and the Blade
(For nothing that's of Fantasy can be a common noun),
With which the Last True King's lost heir will bring the Dark Lord down.

For sons of a republic founded far from tyrant's rule,
Where freedom and equality are pledged each day in school,
Prefer a feudal Kingdom that requires its Rightful Lord
To show his Family Jewels when he unsheathes his Mighty Sword;
Where the war is never over till the Cause of Light is won,
And the One Man Who Could Win It is the Fool Who Couldn't's son.
For blood will out, and heroes always get another chance,
Within the world of wizardry and second-hand romance.

R D Gardner

Knight by Nikola Temkov

Word Weaver II: The Rock of Silence

The Word Weaver stands on the shore
Ready to cast her net
Over the dark brooding rocks
Snaring one, she snags the fragile netting
On dark jagged edges.

The rock is all impenetrable shade
No mellifluous words of colour
No soft ample roundness
In fact the very opposite
A stern precipitous silence
Severe and brutal, slicing the words in two.

Word Weaver tries again
Making her words more malleable
Silky smooth, easy and indulgent
Simple caressing words. Rich and velvety.
The thunderous rock enmeshed in a web
Of delicate promises.

But the Word Weaver cannot live
Without the binding magic of words
Finding the silent rock deaf to her wants
And deaf to her needs.
A rain of words falls upon the rock
Nagging words, harpy words
Biting and painful, incensed petty sounds, vicious and shrill
As cold and sharp as hail.

But the rock shrugs them off into the sea
They hurt, but the rock is mute and immutable.
So is the way between
Weaver and Rock
Words and Silence
Women and Men

Helen Francis

Yellow Leaves

He went into the wood
He stayed too long
Something in the blood
The wood went into him
He came out wrong

He came out wild
At night he runs
Some nights he runs for miles
Some nights he howls
His eyes are yellow now
Like wolves', like owls'
Yet when he smiles
His lover sees the gentleman inside
Inside, he is a gentle man

(They are not lovers, yet
She knew they would be lovers
When they met)

One night, despite the screams,
She dreams -

A dream of leaves
A cloak of yellow leaves
A cloak to cover
Her wounded lover

The wood had harmed him
The wood could heal him

But – it is the dark half of the year
The leaves have left
So she must wait
Wait till next year
For things to grow again
And hope she's not too late

Still here, next year

To find the leaves, she must go deep
The strongest trees, the softest leaves
Deep inside the wood

(She knew she could
For she'd survived, inside
The shadow of the wood)

But – what she needs
Is up so high
Almost out of reach
So she must climb, climb
Climb higher
The bark is sharp
Blood stains her thighs
She doesn't mind

The leaves must not be crushed
They must be whole, untouched
She checks each leaf is right
To match the yellow light
The light behind his eyes
The dark behind the light
Like must meet like

Armloads of leaves
She brings them home
She sits down by the fire
Firelight dancing in her hair
She plucks hairs from her head
Uses them as thread
To sew the cloak
The cloak of yellow leaves

And as she sews the cloak
It seems the seams
Spell out a name
Again and again
Over and over
The name of her lover

Over and over
Again and again
Sewing a spell
Of her lover's name

She hears him howl
Takes the cloak
Goes outside
Into the night

She must be strong
He doesn't want her
Too long he's wandered
On his own, yet still he has his pride
Looks at her with yellow eyes
Glares, dares her to come close
He could rip out her throat

But – she will not leave her love alone
She grabs him
Holds him close
She won't let go
Wraps him in the cloak
The cloak of yellow leaves

Leaves soft as skin
Soft as leather
Sinks right in
Under the skin
Downy soft
Sweet as clover
Sinking into the wounded lover

Yellow leaves
The yellow leaves
The yellow leaves his eyes
The anger dies
He cries

Anne Murphy

...and here he is, himself...

...the cheers and stamping are subsiding and he's saying 'excuse me my
friends, I need time with my friend here, and I'll be back' he's
turning to me and saying, as he draws back the
richly embroidered curtain, 'we can talk in here'

'thank you for giving me of your time, it is so limited' I'm saying
I'm thinking 'oops does he know his fate' he's looking slightly bemused as
he's saying 'yes I'm bard of the summer and then the time of
falling must come' he's pausing with a deep faraway look

'but we are here today' he's saying, as he's slapping me jocundly
on the back 'and you want to talk with me?' I'm noticing his slightly
questioning tone and shyly asking him
'is it okay if I ask you a question?' I'm rushing on
'as I'm writing a poem of you

for a competition' obviously delighted his smile is saying as
his voice is saying 'ask away'
'what was it like' I'm stumbling over my tongue 'inside I mean?'
'inside?' his light quiet tone is coming to me as if from another place

'the deep warmth enveloping me and I emerging from the light,
the nourishing of one who does not want to nourish,
of one who wants to own but not birth, of one
who wants that which labour produces but without labour, of one
who gives but does not want to give,

'inside?' he's pausing but continuing 'I am coming as music filling
the banqueting hall, as story filling the long firelight evening, as salmon
leaping and eating hazelnuts,
as colour flowing out of the one pure light, I am coming...'
he's smiling at me and I'm lost for words

captivated by his voice… 'my lord' I'm almost stuttering 'th th thank you'
I am stuttering, and lightly touching my forehead with the back of my hand
'thank you my lord'
'thank you' he's saying and smiling and lightly touching his forehead
with the back of his hand

'bard sing of me… and I, my friend, will be with you'

my heart is leaping, my awen stirring, my poem…
…Taliesin is turning and going… I'm on my own…
…but not on my own…

Steve Mann

Peredur and the Crystal Cup

by Caroline Clark

Once upon a time there was a king who had one son called Peredur. He was the joy of his father's heart and a good-natured, gentle young man. Although he had many friends he liked nothing better than to ride alone through the royal forests or sit beside the river until birds and beasts had no fear of him. The king thought that Peredur should marry so he often invited the royal and noble daughters of his peers to banquets and festivals. Peredur was charming to all but charmed by none. The queen of a kingdom to the east of his own was determined that he should marry her daughter and sent her in gowns as gorgeous as the sun but Peredur scarcely seemed to see her. She danced with him till her feet bled in her golden shoes but when the dances were over he turned politely away with no word of love.

One day he slipped away from court and followed the river until he came to a clearing he had not found before. In it there was a fountain and beside this sat a girl. Her robes seemed as soft and graceful as the water and her bright hair cascaded over her shoulders. She welcomed him to sit by her and they talked happily until evening came and he had to return. He asked her to visit him but she only said: "If you want to find me, here I will be."

Peredur returned next day and for many days. He forgot all other company and lived only to be with her whom he called Sildyn. At last he begged her to marry him. She told him that her father would not let her go unless the man who loved her was brave enough to take the treasure which was at the heart of the fountain and faithful enough to keep any promise she asked of him. Peredur said that he feared nothing except losing her and with that he reached into the fountain.

Instantly the water became dark, steaming blood, blinding and choking him. He fought for breath but reached further in. Then he could see nothing but raging fire, flames engulfed him and the flesh seemed to melt from his bones but he grasped something smooth and hard under his hand and drew it out. All around fell cool water, his skin bore no stain and in his hand was a cup like a five-petalled flower made of crystal. The girl ran to him and kissed him with great joy.

"So long as you keep this safe I will be yours, but you must promise one thing: I will always tell you the truth but if you ask me something twice and I do not reply, never ask me a third time or you will lose me and all I bring to you."

Peredur promised gladly and they went together to his father. The king so loved his son and was so charmed by Sildyn's beauty that he gave his consent and they were married. The nobles and rulers who were his guests could not discover where this princess had sprung from but, as the match favoured none of their rivals, all seemed happy enough. Only the eastern queen seethed with jealousy at her daughter's loss. She presented the pair with rich gifts and among them a servant girl to sing to the princess (and keep the queen well informed).

For a year Peredur and Sildyn lived happily together until the time drew near when she would bear a child. She told Peredur that she must go into the forest alone. He feared for her and asked where she would go but she gave no answer. He asked if she would take no-one with her and again she was silent, so he let her go. A month later she returned with a daughter and their happiness together was greater than ever.

After another year events followed the same course. Sildyn left her daughter with the old nurse who had cared for Peredur. She parted tenderly from her husband and went into the forest. A month later she returned with another fair daughter and all was well with them. The girls grew as graceful and bright-faced as their mother. They were the darlings of the old king who seemed to grow younger every time he played with them. But others looked on them with stranger eyes.

The singing girl from the east had been much in demand for her music and visited many noble households. From these began a whispering. Some made signs against evil when Sildyn or her girls were near and fewer children were brought to court. Peredur's friends loved them for his sake but they began to ask about Sildyn's lineage and who had attended her daughters' births.

When the younger daughter was three years old, Sildyn was again carrying a child. Peredur asked her to stay with him but she said she must go, nor would she take any company but slipped away one evening. That night some of his friends came with grave faces. They began urging that the princess should be guarded for her own protection. Then came a darker tale – that she had been followed before by a servant who had seen her give birth to a monster. Her daughters were children stolen or bought from poor peasants. Peredur mocked them and asked how changelings could be so like their foster mother.

"Witchcraft." they said.

Peredur sent them away but in his mind he saw the fountain of blood and flame. He went to his bed-chamber where the crystal cup was kept in a secret cabinet. He opened the hidden doors and took it in his hands. Even in the candle-light it sparkled like a star, perfect and pure. He replaced it. He felt in his heart no doubt of Sildyn but he began to fear that others would do her harm. If he followed her alone no-one could slander her again without reproof. He wrapped himself in his dark cloak and set off, swift and silent, to the fountain glade. He found no other watchers there and at first thought he had overtaken Syldin in the forest. Then, as he watched, the fountain began to glimmer with a pearly light. Out of it rose Sildyn carrying a naked child. Peredur was so happy that he ran towards them but before he reached the pool of light he saw her bend and plunge the child into water which turned to fire. Forgetting that the flames of his ordeal had not burned him, Peredur cried out.

"Sildyn! What have you done? What are you? Why will you kill our son?"

The child which had till then been quiet began to scream. Sildyn snatched him to her and leapt from the fountain which returned to water.

"What have *You* done?" she cried. "You have lost us all!"

Peredur looked at the baby. It was perfect in everything except on his back was a dark scar, the shape of a tear, where a drop from the fire-fountain had burned him.

"You have asked me three questions and now I will answer you. I am the child of a great spirit: master of sea and earthquake, of whose kingdom this fountain is a gateway. I returned to my father so that my children could be born through water and fire and could not be harmed by them. Your fear almost killed your son. If you had trusted me and had the courage which won me, all would have been well. Now you will never find us again unless what is broken and scattered is made whole."

Peredur threw his arms round Sildyn and the child, crying out that she must not leave him, but they melted and flowed away through his hands like a stream of water. He could not hold them and stood alone in the dark glade.

Suddenly there was a terrible grinding roar deep in the earth. The ground twisted and flung him down, shuddering under his hands, tearing like cloth. The fountain vanished as a ravine opened before him. Trees crashed around him and he seemed to see a huge dark shape, crowned and edged with blue fire, rise to blot out the sky.

Peredur woke to the shouts of his huntsmen. He was battered and half buried but able to move. He called out for Sildyn but no-one had seen her and when he saw the riven earth he remembered and wept. He rode furiously back to the palace and burst into the nursery but one look at the old woman's stricken face confirmed his fears. The girls had vanished in the night at the moment the earthquake shook the palace. Peredur went to his chamber and opened the secret door but instead of the crystal flower he found only a single petal lying like a tear on the velvet. He crumpled to his knees, too stunned even to weep, until his nurse came and began to clean and bathe his hurts as she had done when he was a child. She drew from him all that had happened, then she said: "You must find what is lost."

"How can I find the four drops in the ocean that are mine, if the sea itself swallows them up." He cried.

"You have one piece left of the crystal cup, if you can make that whole again I believe Sildyn will return. Seek out the gates of her father's kingdom. It may be those who keep them can help you."

The king was horrified when Peredur told him the quest he was undertaking and said: "If I have lost my grandchildren, must I lose you too? What will become of the kingdom if you do not return? If the gods have taken back their gifts you must be content. There are mortal women enough who will love you."

But Peredur said: "Let me go, with your blessing, for the kingdom's sake, for I will have no other wife."

Then he made ready and rode away, carrying the broken petal close to his heart.

23

He travelled wherever he heard an earthquake had opened the earth and sought for news or story that would lead him to a keeper of the gate. At last he came to a cavern where men said there lived an ancient earth-snake which knew many secrets. He climbed down into the dark where rocks had been pulled apart but he felt that at any moment they might clamp together again and crush him to powder. He struggled on until his hands met a wall on which he felt the coiled, ribbed shape of a huge serpent of stone. He could go no further. Surely there was nothing here that could help him? Then he saw a point of crimson light, as if an eye had opened. He whispered: "Earthlord have mercy. Tell me what I must do to find what I have lost."

At first there was no sound but the beating of his own heart. Then a voice, so deep that he felt it in his bones rather than heard it, said: "The path is long; through earth, water, fire and time. Take what you have won, if you dare."

Peredur felt the coils of the snake loosen so that he could put his hand into their centre and there he felt a small, smooth shape. He gripped it and drew out his hand before the coils tightened again. Then he crawled out towards the mouth of the cave and saw that he held a petal which sparkled in the moonlight.

He travelled south until he came to the shore where great breakers roared against grey cliffs. The people who lived there told him of an ancient turtle which they believed was a messenger of the lord of the sea. If a man dared to seize and ride him he might reach his master. Peredur's heart sank when they showed him a domed rock which, at low tide, appeared as big as a hill. He climbed it, slimy and barnacled, with only the weathered crown clear of weed. The stone was cracked into huge plates which did resemble a turtle's shell but how could he dream that it could ever move, let alone swim?

Night and day he waited on the rock, only leaving it at low tide to get food. His skin became brown and scorched by salt wind and his clothes like the tattered weed. The only sign of his princely life were his rings and the locket at his throat holding his two fragments of hope. One night there was a fearful storm, waves crashed and tore even over the crown of the island. Peredur clung like a limpet, his fingers and toes wedged into the rock seams. Then he felt a shudder beneath him. He feared another earthquake but the motion became more regular: a slow surging up and down. The storm quietened and it seemed to him that the dome of the island rose and fell against the stars.

As dawn broke he could doubt no more, no land was to be seen behind him. Inch by inch he crawled to the top of the rock and looked ahead. The broad prow of stone was speeding through the waves and ahead was something which now and then appeared like a smaller island, or a very large scaly head. For many hours the turtle swam steadily until Peredur saw, outlined against the setting sun, a thin dark line. Through the night he could not judge how far they advanced although, by the stars, he guessed that the turtle had not changed direction. At dawn he saw white surf below a line of cliffs and began to hear a hollow roar but there was no sign of a beach on which to land. The turtle showed no sign of turning. Peredur did all he could to anchor toes and fingers in the rock cracks and took a deep breath just as it began to dive. He clung among the seaweed, seeing green light grow fainter but the blackness was in his own eyes.

He lost his hold and shot to the surface, choking. For a few moments it seemed that he could suddenly breathe water for he was in a cavern filled with blue, wavy light. Light came from below him and he floated on the surface of a sea within a mountain. He righted himself and could dimly see there were walls on either side. As he swam towards one his heart lifted with joy for there were people at the water's edge, white arms reached out to him. For a while he believed his wife and daughters called to him. Then a wave lifted him higher and he saw a host like women, tall and pale. Long dark ribbons of weed cloaked them and in the arms of some were clasped parcels of bleached bones.

He veered away and swam deeper into the mountain, although that took him further from the light. Behind him rose a high, hungry keening which faded into the distance. He swam on, almost without hope, until he thought he saw a pale patch of light, not blue as the light behind him. Soon he could see it was indeed daylight, falling through a narrow chimney of rock. He found he could pull himself onto a sort of wall, just below the surface, and stand.

25

Forgetting his quest he reached up, thinking only of escaping to the world above, when a pebble, dislodged, fell into the water and he looked down along the light as it pierced the clear, still depths. He was looking into a shaft, an under-water well whose depth he could not guess, but at its base was a star.

At first Peredur dived and tried to swim down, he clawed at the sides but could not force himself deep enough. Then he climbed onto the wall again. Above him the cavern roof was rough. He could prise out a large rock and sink with it into the well, but that might mean he could not climb up into the chimney. He longed for light and air but if he failed in his quest he did not care where or how he died. He tore the rock free, clutched it and fell. He sank to the foot of the shaft and carefully reached out towards the crystal petal, though his chest was bursting and the blackness crept back behind his eyes. Then, holding it tightly in one hand, he released his hold on the rock-anchor and launched himself upwards. For a long while he rested on the rock wall, securing his treasure with its fellows and regaining his strength. He made some attempts to pull himself up into the cleft but could reach nothing that would bear his weight. He stretched out his hands over the water and said: "Lord of the Sea, I have dared your depths, release me to face the fire."

At first all was still, then he heard an echoing roar, a blast of air knocked him over and he was in a swirling maelstrom as a huge wave raced through the cavern, caught him and tossed him up through the shaft. He felt ledges on either side and jammed his feet and arms into them. Then as the water was sucked back he put out all his remaining strength. When his head cleared he was still wedged high in the chimney and he began slowly and painfully to climb.

By the time he had reached the surface it was dark. He sensed that he was on an open hillside but was too weary to do more than drag himself clear of the shaft before he fell into a deep sleep. Waking, he found half a dozen small faces peering into his. He leapt up and shouted in fear but they were only a band of dark-haired children who scattered squealing with laughter and soon came back. He could not make out their words, though they did sound a little familiar, but easily made them understand that he needed food. They ran off down the hill and soon returned with a small, dark woman carrying a basket.

Peredur bowed to her and made signs to reassure her that he was no danger. Indeed she soon saw that he was not only hungry but covered in bruises and wounds so, when he had eaten and drunk, she helped him down to her home and gave him a bed in the loft over the stable.

There she cared for him until he grew strong again. He learned a little of the language, helped on the farm and played with the children. Peredur found that he was in the kingdom to the east of his own (whose queen had so courted him for her daughter). When he asked his hostess if there was a fiery mountain in their country she said she had never seen such a thing but her husband, who was a soldier and had been sent to the northern border, had told them of one under which a dragon lay and spouted fire – but she had not believed him. Peredur said he must find it but she was loath to let him go. When he told her his story she was amazed but, seeing he was a prince and under the command of so great a power, could not delay him. She gave him food, clothes and a sword left by her husband, she also warned him that the Queen's soldiers would seize him if he came too near her city. He was sorry to leave her and to part from her children who had brought back happy memories of his own. He gave her a gold ring stamped with his father's crest and said that if any of her family needed help in *his* kingdom they should show this ring. Then he set off northwards to find the mountain of fire.

After a few days he found a group of merchants travelling that way and was taken on as a porter. He said little and trudged on unregarded until their way became steep and sharp peaks appeared in the distance. He began to draw from travellers who joined the group stories of the mountain country. One day the porters of an old merchant who had camped near Peredur told him that their master lived below a mountain which was always capped with cloud and sometimes spat fire into the night. They did not wish to go near it and Peredur bargained with them so that they changed masters and he carried the old man's goods instead. The merchant was surly at first but when Peredur had shown himself strong and faithful (catching and riding back a valuable horse which had escaped) he began to tell him about their destination.

The mountain, he said, was sacred to the Earthlord and people spoke of a dragon guardian but he had often been onto its slopes to collect the precious black glass he traded in and had come to no harm. He promised to show Peredur the shrine as soon as he had stored his goods safely. A few days later they climbed the lower slopes and came to a place where water ran hot from the earth, strange mudpools pulsed as if the land was breathing and foul-smelling smoke came from a cave mouth. Here brave men came with questions and wicked ones were brought for judgement; for those who entered the cave either dreamed true dreams or died.

Peredur wrapped his cloak around his face and walked into the smoke. It was hot, dark and stifling but he felt his way forward to the end of the cleft where there was an altar. He placed his hands on it and said: "Earthlord, I am in your hand, give me back your daughter or destroy me."

Then he staggered out into the light, lay down by the grey pool and fell into a deep sleep.

To Peredur, however, it seemed that he fell not beside the pool but into it. Blind, deaf, unbreathing, he sank into the ooze, aware only of waves of unbearable heat. He settled at last on burning rock and opened his eyes to find he stood upright in a clear pool of liquid fire. Before him was a shimmering figure, poised in the element as a vast shoal of golden fish catches the light as they turn and swirl. Light became robes, a crown and finally eyes of white heat, which seared into his own. Knowing that what he saw was impossible, he stammered out: "Lord, how can this be?" and heard:

"In spirit you must fight my firedrake.
Fear and you fail; fail and you will not wake."

Then the vision dissolved and Peredur moved forward through the pool. He found himself on the edge of a crater in which magma seethed and now and then he glimpsed the crest or tail of a huge creature, swimming there. As he watched it reared a scaly head, white heat spewed from its jaws but on its brow was a point of diamond brightness. He felt in his hand a sword, (it seemed the sword the soldier's wife had given him, though true metal would have boiled away in that place) at his throat he touched the familiar shape of gold which held his hard-won tokens.

"All on one throw!" he cried and leaped down onto the dragon's head. As in the fountain long ago, he seemed to feel the flesh shrivel from his bones as the wildfire licked around him. He stabbed the sword into its hide but felt it twitch as if at a fleabite. Pain, which seemed real beyond any imagining, maddened him but he clung on as the beast shook its crest. He slid forward and almost to save himself falling, drove his sword down into the socket of the eye. There was a spurt of blood, blinding him like acid, then the dragon sank down, a floating hulk. Peredur clawed his way back to the brow and in the centre was a small, smooth jewel which he cut out by touch alone. He clutched it in his hand, letting the sword drop and said: "Father, is it enough?"

Then his spirit knew no more until there stole upon him a soft voice singing and he knew that it was Sildyn. He opened his eyes to find himself in a cool glade, like that in his own forest. He lay bathed by the water of a fountain and in the arms of his wife. Two graceful girls played nearby and when he called to them they ran and kissed him and clung to his hands. But Peredur asked Sildyn: "Has your father relented? Have we come home?"

Sildyn held him tightly and caressed him but could not speak for a while, then she said: "Your body still sleeps beside the mountain pool and when you wake you still have to travel the road home, but never doubt that we will be with you, even if you do not always see us. You have broken the locks of all his kingdoms and not even my father can keep us apart again. But the flower had five petals; one is still lost and only time will find our son."
Peredur cried: "If this is dreaming let me never wake. Better live here with you, whatever world this is, than wake alone."

But Sildyn shook her head: "I cannot hold a dream," she said.

Then as he reached out to her he felt the cool water become hot, dusty earth and his eyes opened on the court of the fire-mountain. His despair was so bitter that he almost cast himself into the sulphurous pool but he remembered her words and opened the locket. There were four petals. Peredur returned to the merchant's house and offered his last ring for a horse, then he rode as fast as he

29

could for the border of his own kingdom. After many days he reached a ridge which overlooked the river dividing the kingdoms. There was a ford, heavily guarded, where all travellers were examined and sometimes robbed by the soldiers. Peredur knew that he had only one thing of value on him and he would kill an army rather than lose it now, if that were the only way to clear the road. He looked at the water and remembered Sildyn's promise so he called out: "Lady of the water, wash my way clear."

As he galloped towards the ford he saw a high wave race downstream. The men at the crossing scrambled away from the water and, in the moment after it passed the ford, Peredur splashed through the shallows. He was seized by the guards on the western side but when he said: "Take me to the king, I am Peredur, his son."

They cheered. They told him the king had sent word to keep watch for his coming and would reward them. They had thought it the madness of an old man, since it was so long since the prince had vanished, but now all would be well. Peredur, dressed in new clothes and with a fresh horse, was escorted by the guards to his palace where the old king embraced him with such mingled joy and grief that Peredur feared he would die of it. The king told him how, a few nights ago, Sildyn's daughters had appeared to him and told him Peredur would return.

The next day they rode together into the forest. Trees had sprung up to shade the ravine and into it flowed a stream from the broken rocks. Peredur lifted his father down from his horse and they knelt beside the water. At first they saw only sunlight dancing on the surface, then Peredur reached out his arms as Sildyn rose like a salmon leaping and they danced together for pure joy. The girls rose to embrace the old king and they all returned to the palace where feasting and celebration greeted them.

When Peredur had told his adventures and learnt from his father how the kingdom had been faring, he set himself to serve them faithfully. In a few years the old king died, content that all was well. Peredur and Sildyn ruled in his place and the land prospered. Crops were never blighted by drought; rich harvests from land and sea made their people strong; gold glittering in many mountain streams made them wealthy. The princesses were loved by all; Peredur took them with him and taught them the duties of a ruler. Only with Sildyn did he ever speak of their son.

In the kingdom to the east the old queen died. Her daughter, a fierce and bitter woman, heard every day of the riches of King Peredur. She strengthened her army, not least to stop her subjects drifting away to his kingdom for many had already done so. Any attempt to raid across the border failed as if the land itself resisted her: rivers rose, swamps swallowed her forces, storms dispersed her ships of war. She knew well that Sildyn's powers were great but she called on powers of her own and gazed into the dark. There she saw a young man: a soldier of fortune who led a loyal band in search of wealth and glory. One aspect above all intrigued her: they called him Gwern for it was said water could not harm him.

She sent messengers to him with rich gifts and richer promises and soon he marched into her city like a conqueror, splendid in crimson and gold and at his throat hung a sparkling gem. When she looked in his face she was cast into turmoil for it was the face of Peredur when, years ago, she had desired him and he had turned away.

Gwern listened to the story of her army's failures then he laughed: "If I lead them they'll stay dry enough, but what will you give me in return?"

The queen's eyes glittered as she said: "Seize for me the province with the golden rivers and you can reign with me over all my lands and be my lord."

Gwern was surprised that she offered so much but he gave her his word and set about winning the confidence of her army. When he had called together forces from all corners of the kingdom he mustered them in a broad river valley and ordered them to cross the torrent. They hung back but he walked into the river and his own men followed him, the water lapping at their ankles, soft as wool. The queen's men cheered and rushed in after him, eager now to follow wherever he led.

Some weeks later a man was brought to Peredur by guards who said he had word for the king and bore his ring. Peredur did not know him but he said: "My mother sent me, she cared for you and would not have me die fighting to steal your land."

Then he told Peredur of the new general and all he had seen in the valley.

That night Peredur and Sildyn talked far into the night. Their first duty was to protect their people but hope they hardly dared to name made them long to see the very man who threatened their kingdom.

Peredur sent a herald to the queen's general asking to meet him, under truce, at an island in the river. Gwern (who never wasted his men) was glad, hoping the threat was enough to gain him ground, but the queen would not hear of it. She warned him of Sildyn's magic and feared he would betray her. So Gwern sent back word that he would meet the king on the island but only in combat of champions and if he won his army would occupy the eastern province. Peredur agreed for he said: "If he is my son all will be well; if not, I must kill him."

The next day Peredur set out for the island alone in a small boat. He carried shield, armour, spear and sword. When Gwern saw that he had alighted and made ready he marched fully armed into the river, strode across and took guard on the shore. From the moment he saw his enemy's face, Peredur had no doubt: he saw what he had been. Gwern saw only what he might become – a king. Peredur sheathed his sword and called out: "Let it be peace, not war, between us, for you are my son."

But Gwern pressed on towards him for the queen had told him Peredur would try to enthral him with spells and she had sealed his ears with wax. The fight raged to and fro along the strand for both were swift and skilful, but where Gwern was bent on victory Peredur sought always to defend, not to wound and was steadily driven towards the water. Gwern pressed on, sure of his advantage, until Peredur fell, hampered by the drag of the current. The sword scythed down towards his throat. Suddenly Gwern was caught up in a swirl of water and swept backwards onto the shore but found the wave change to the clinging arms of three women. He roared with rage and hacked at them with his sword but the blade met only water. He cursed them for witches and Peredur for a coward but Sildyn held him fast with the strength of a tide-race. The girls pulled off the silver chain on which hung the shining petal. Peredur struggled back to them and, opening the golden locket on his own breast, took out the other four.

Gwern was amazed and ceased to struggle as Peredur laid the five pieces of crystal on the earth.

> "Earth, water, fire and time are past,
> Earth-father make us one at last!"

As they watched there rose a pillar of fiery light above the flower. The petals sparkled until not even Sildyn could endure their brightness and all hid their faces. The wax melted and Gwern too heard a voice from the heart of the fire:

> "What's won with love and bitter pain
> Not fire nor flood shall part again."

When they dared to look up they saw the crystal cup, made whole, lay between them. Gwern knelt before it and said: "Tell me what this means and who you are that I have fought against."

Then Sildyn and Peredur told him all that had happened and he was full of joy to find so noble a father. They called both their armies to the banks of the river and Peredur proclaimed that Gwern, his son, should become regent of the province of golden rivers. There should be peace between the kingdoms and the people of the east would share in the prosperity of his own. At this there was great rejoicing on all sides but the Queen rode to Gwern and screamed that he had betrayed her. He replied: "I fought in good faith and served your people well, though you would have made me kill my own father. I will not hold you to your promise, nor share your kingdom."

She looked from him to Peredur then she turned and rode silently away through the ranks of her jubilant army.

The queen shut herself away in her palace with a bitter heart and would see no-one. When her chamberlains broke down the door they found her lying dead, wrapped in a gown which still shone like the sun.

The people of the east called for Gwern to rule them so the two kingdoms prospered side by side and on the arms of each there is a crystal cup, the jewel and treasure of the house.

33

Unicorn

Long long time ago
and far far away,
I once loved a maiden
forever and a day;
until she found a magic unicorn
and on it rode away.

Though I cried a thousand years
I really could not say,
if not for that unicorn,
I could have made her stay.

Derek Adams

Did you hear the sword sing?

Was there a moment of silence -
between the laughs of derision
and the roar of the crowd?

Did you hear the sword sing
with the voice of an angel,
the sound of iron against steel
as it slid from the anvil?

Were you as surprised
as Sir Kay's wide open eyes
or as knowing as Merlin,
when you touched the hilt,
felt the power - the unity?

Derek Adams

Dreams, visions, reflections
of The Lady of Shalott

In a sacred place of sanctuary, close to Camelot
I met with owl and hawk,
flew high above wold and tree-tops,
not in my worldly garb
   but cloaked in feathers, eyes keen –
      constellations above me, stretching out forever.
Such freedom I had never known.
Far below me, a camp of wise and spiritual ones.
I knew the magic of their grove
the inner world and invisible world.

As I sit by my window
I feel the power of the Goddess,
   when moon reflected is full and globed
      and with the sickle
the hoot of the owl calls, she speaks
of many heart questions

In woods, across the fields of gold,
I felt the energy of life.
There, I found a hidden pool and from its depths
I heard the whisper '*Lancelot*'.
From that same water
in the reflections
   of aspen, birch and willow –
      rose the man of the woods.
Green in name
his colour was not the vision for me
but his face decked in leaves resplendent.

So cruel the dreams where
I may pluck the fragrant lilies
  whose scent I know so well,
    touch their pure white petals, soft so soft.
  or run my hands through cooling waters
trailed by my beloved willows

One night the white horse came
eyes wild yet gentle
his desire to take me
   on a journey
      of knowledge and wisdom
to the land of crystal towers and soaring mountains.
I was not ready then,
my weaving not yet done, my web-story unfinished.
I will be ready soon, so the cloaked one told me
then, the mirror will no longer hold my world.
When the time is right
I will clamber on the stallion's back
…and fly free

Sally Richards

Oh to be Silver

I'm free-floating, silver bubbles
star bursting against my skin.
I watch them burst and flatten
like phosphorescent fish scales –
no, no, the sheen is more reminiscent
of a mermaid
in Diana's silvered moonlight.
Silver surfing on the outgoing tide
of the silver streak,
drifting to I know not where.
I taste salt crystals on dappled tongue,
and dream of distant shores –
of spices, soaring minarets,
sumptuous brocades,
lapis lazuli sky offering
serious sunshine to penetrate tissue and bone.
Breath is crystallising
in soporific glacial shapes
juxtaposed with the experience,
the here and now of crisp cold waves,
of cooling blood, and lips of marble.
Eyes blinking against the speed
of shooting stars
as I search and search for a silver lining
in the fading range
of clotted clouds.
I suspect, as this heart,
this brain, stumbles and slows,
that I will not find what I seek.
I know I will not reach
those hazy sun dappled shores.
I will not see that vision,
ensuring it remains euphoric Utopia.

I will hear no more vacuous voices,
no star-spangled songs.
But this drifting silence
in an endless pearled horizon
seems almost preferable to the
falsity of silver-speech and honeyed tones.
Oh, to be silver tongued
in the next apocalyptic world.

Dee Gordon

Silver Stream

by Caroline Clark

Once upon a time a knight and his lady had three daughters whom they loved dearly. The eldest girl had eyes that danced like stars mirrored in the sea; the second, tall and queenly, had hair golden as ripe corn and their mother was proud of their beauty. The youngest, a little brown bird of a child, was easy to pass over in her sisters' shadow but her father was never happier than when he listened to her chatter and, because of her sweet voice, he called her his silver stream.

The time came when the king summoned his knights to war. The lord of the castle was grieved to leave his home, but he made ready his men, took up his great silver-hilted sword and sadly parted from his lady. To his eldest daughter he gave a necklace of diamonds, to the second a golden collar. The youngest girl clung to him and would not be comforted with the silver chain he put about her neck. He set her down, saying, "Let this keep you company till I come again" and gave her a singing bird in a silver cage. Then he rode out of the castle gate, between the glinting stubble fields and into the forest.

Midwinter was cheerless with no word of him. Months passed, the bird sang sadly and Silver Stream grew silent. Her mother attended to the life of the castle faithfully and watched the road in vain. Winter came again. Out of the dark trees rode a young knight under the king's banner and men marched with him but behind him came a wagon bearing a black-draped coffin and a silver-hilted sword.

The king's messenger knelt before the lady and told his tale of courage and death. He had been sent to bring home his brother-in-arms and serve her as best he could. She wept for her husband and he was buried in the castle chapel where his great sword hung above his tomb. Sir Lycias, the king's servant, was courteous and kind. He managed all as the lady wished and charmed the elder girls with his grace. Silver Stream chose to sleep in a little room beside the chapel. She hid away in her grief, talking to her bird until she fancied it talked to her. After a year and a day Sir Lycias spoke of returning to court but the lady pressed him to stay and soon grew in love with him. He courted her gallantly and swore to hold her daughters dear as his own flesh. In spring they were married and the pretty daughters danced at the wedding but Silver Stream would not leave her room. Sir Lycias came to plead tenderly with her but the bird shrieked at him. He put his hand on the cage and snatched it away as if the silver had been red-hot iron. Soon after, he rode off to do homage to the king for the lordship of the castle, but he promised to return on May morning.

The bright-eyed eldest girl was crowned with garlands, Queen of the May. Eager to impress her handsome step-father, she begged her mother to let her ride to meet him. The forest edge was white with blossom as she rode in with her young friends but Silver Stream did not go with them for, as she made ready, the bird sang:

"Stay, mistress, stay,
Or you'll come not back today".

Sir Lycias arrived home and greeted his wife. He said he had seen no sign of the girls on the road. Alarmed, a party set out and were met by a doleful sight: the village girls returning in tears, carrying the body of their queen. They told how they had no sooner entered the forest when a great grey wolf leapt out. The girl's pony bolted, pursued by the wolf and when they found her she was dead. Sir Lycias swore to destroy the beast and hunted it day after day but they found neither the wolf nor the necklace it had torn from her throat. The young knight and his grieving lady mourned the girl and laid her beside her father while the sisters comforted one another. A year went by; Sir Lycias was high in the king's favour, wearing a fine jewelled sword belt, a present from court. The fields spread, golden with grain, below the castle and the sisters joined the villagers to bring in the harvest. On the last day Silver Stream was about to go down when her bird sang:

"Stay, mistress, stay,
Or you'll come not back today".

She told her sister that they were in danger and should stay at home, but the golden-haired girl would not listen. She was to be queen of the feast so she mocked her little sister for being jealous and ran to her friends. At the end of the day she rode on the last wagon bringing the harvest home when suddenly, running swiftly as a grey shadow, a great wolf leapt into the midst of the reapers. It grabbed the girl and was away, chased by the villagers, into the forest.

How bitterly all lamented her loss! Sir Lycias found her torn gown but little of her body remained, not even her golden collar. The young lord lovingly comforted his lady and she turned only to him, almost forgetting her youngest child who was now so much alone. The year turned and another drew into autumn. Sir Lycias proposed that he should take Silver Stream to court to become a lady in waiting for he said: "Here she pines for her sisters and will never get a husband."

Her mother thought this was wise and Silver Stream made ready.

That night the bird sang to her:

"Bright the jewels on his sword,
Fair the gold upon his arm,
Mistress, do not trust his word
Or you'll come to mortal harm."

Silver Stream begged that she should not leave before All Hallows when she should pray for her father and her mother agreed to this although Sir Lycias was not pleased.

On All Hallows Eve she was woken by the bird's shrieking. She heard a scratching and tearing at her door and fled into the chapel. Close at her heels in the darkness she felt the breath of the beast. She screamed for her father as its jaws closed on her neck. Then the wolf jerked away, the silver chain she wore had touched its tongue. The girl leapt onto the tomb, seized the great sword and plunged it into the wolf's mouth. The body fell to the ground and in a shaft of moonlight she saw Sir Lycias, dead at her feet, his teeth clenched on the silver hilt of her father's sword.

The Good Knight and the Castle of the Bears

by Douglas Bruton

Once there was a good knight and he was on a journey, a quest for adventure. His only company was a great white horse on which the good knight carried all that he possessed in the world – though this did not amount to very much.

It was winter and everywhere the snow fell in large soft flakes. The wind blew bitter cold, picking up the snow and driving it into the face of the good knight making it difficult for him to see more than a short way in front of his painfully numb feet. The cold reached under his thick clothes and caressed his skin with icy fingers.

The good knight, his head bent and one arm raised protectively against the biting blast, led the great white horse slowly across the unmarked snow, its iron-shod hooves slipping clumsily on the hard frozen earth. There was panic in the horse's eyes and with each stumble it whinnied and snorted wildly, pulling on the reins so that the good knight had to keep stopping to pat its neck in reassurance. He whispered comforting clicks and clacks into its bent ears. Behind them the tracks they made were quickly erased so that they could neither say where they had been nor where they were going.

Suddenly the wind dropped in front of them, though they could still hear it whistling shrilly at their backs. The good knight wiped the crust of snow from his brow and looking up discovered that they were standing in the lee of a towering castle wall, which effectively blocked their path and sheltered them from the bitter wind. In the centre of the wall and a short way to the right of where the good knight stood there was a grand entrance. Tall magnificently carved stone statues of giant knights-at-arms flanked a large oak-beamed door coated with pitch and studded over with iron bolts. The good knight approached the entrance and with his fist beat a feeble tattoo on the solid wooden door. There was no reply. The good knight stooped to pick up a rock and balancing it in one hand he hammered three booming knocks on the great oak door, calling at the same time to be admitted to the castle.

All at once he heard the clanking of metal against metal, followed by the dull tread and gruff grunts of gate guards roused from their rest and racing into action. A jangle of heavy chains and the slow creak of swollen wood scraping against stone signalled the opening of the large oak door. It opened only wide enough to admit the good knight and his great white horse. An unlit enclosed passageway led from the outer door to the inner castle wall and a second, less imposing entrance. As soon as the good knight was beyond the outer door he was in almost total darkness. The rattle of the chains and the scraping of the door as it closed behind him sounded ominously bleak.

The great white horse pulled back from the second door in alarm, but before the good knight could turn to steady the animal, strong rough paws pinned his arms to his sides and he was half carried and half pushed along the dark passageway and through the second door. The good knight struggled to break free but he was held fast in a grip of iron. He could hear his horse still shut in the passageway kicking blindly at the walls.

Once through the second door the good knight was pushed on through a third where his eyes were briefly dazzled by the glare of a thousand candles that lit up a vast hall. Tall shadowy figures closed in on the good knight, pawing and pushing him and grunting disapproval. As his eyes adjusted to the bright light, the good knight could see that he was surrounded on all sides by an army of bears.

The two that held his arms locked at his sides marched him through the crowded hall to the end furthest away from the entrance. There on a raised platform and slumped in a splendid gilded throne sat a huge black bear, its massive head supported on a great paw tipped with dagger-like claws. The angle of the black bear's head prevented the good knight from seeing its eyes, but from the slow rise and fall of the bear's chest and the breathy rattle that issued from its shiny pink flared nostrils he suspected that the bear might be asleep. The bears at his side forced him down into a kneeling position at the edge of the platform and then withdrew two paces.

The rest of the bears gathered in the hall began a slow rhythmic grunting, almost like a chant, increasing quickly to a deafening volume so that the walls of the great chamber groaned and the brightly coloured glass in the high windows shook. The good knight covered his ears with his hands.

Slowly the great black bear on its throne raised its enormous head and opened its jaws in a terrifying yawn. The gruff chant ended suddenly, as if this were a prearranged and carefully rehearsed signal. The great black bear settled its paws on the arms of the throne, pulled itself into an upright position and blinked its eyes until they focussed on the kneeling good knight with his hands still covering his ears.

The good knight sensed that the chanting had ceased, despite the loud ringing in his head. He lowered his hands and looked up at the black bear seated on the throne. The bear leaned its huge head towards the good knight and opened its mouth as if speaking confidentially to him. The bear was so close to him that he could see the blotchy brown-stained whites of its eyes, and the stench of its stale breath felt warm on his face and made him want to turn away. But the good knight knew that he could not do this.

At first he could not hear any sound that the bear made for the loud ringing in his ears persisted. But gradually its soft throaty murmur filtered through so that the good knight heard the bear repeat, 'What do you want in the Castle of the Bears?'

The good knight swallowed hard before answering. 'I am a simple knight. I mean you no harm, truly. The blinding snow has so thoroughly dulled my sense of direction and time that I neither know where I am nor what time of the day it is. I beg you for shelter for myself and my horse until the weather weakens and we can resume our journey.'

The good knight was not sure, but it seemed to him that a gruff chuckle issued from the black bear's mouth. The bear made a series of grunts accompanied by a confusion of sweeping gestures with its large paws. The assembled bears seemed to understand and answered with an assortment of barks and coughs.

The black bear looked again into the eyes of the good knight and the hall fell silent once more.

'You and your horse may rest the night here, but we will expect a service from you in return,' the bear growled showing its sharp yellow teeth.

The good knight was unable to reply, but nodded energetically.

'When the sun next begins its passage through the sky you will travel on foot back to the hills you have just crossed. You will climb the hill that is in the shape of a resting lion until you find the black pool of water that lies between the lion's shoulders. In this pool there is a fish. I want that fish. Bring me that fish and I will release you and your horse and you can leave the Castle of the Bears unharmed. My army will watch you closely and if you attempt to escape without fulfilling your end of the bargain they will ride forth from the castle and hunt you down. And you and your horse will never be seen beyond these castle walls again.'

Its explanation at an end the bear rested back in its throne, its eyes still fastened on the good knight.

The silence that followed was not quite complete; the bears in the hall seemed to breathe in unison and as one so that the air in the hall trembled in a low droning hum that rose and fell giving the good knight the unsettling impression that he knelt undigested in the belly of a great beast. The black bear yawned again, though this time it seemed affected and deliberate. It leaned forward and said in a low menacing growl, 'Well, simple knight, do you agree?'

The good knight nodded his agreement. The black bear rose from his throne and addressed the army of bears with open arms, its huge padded paws waving excitedly back and forth. The hall immediately erupted in a booming roar that extinguished some of the candles and brought a fine shower of dust from the roof beams overhead. But before the good knight could shield his ears with his hands he felt his arms pinned to his sides again and he was lifted from his kneeling position and dragged out of the hall.

It was dark outside the great chamber and, like the snow, the darkness disoriented the good knight as he was hauled roughly this way and that through a labyrinthine maze of corridors until they arrived at last at a small windowless room. Two lanterns, sooty and black, hung outside the room on either side of the door, their flames flickering low and throwing out a weak light that was visible only by virtue of the total darkness that blocked out the corridor in every direction. The good knight was thrust forcefully into the room and the door slammed shut. From inside he heard two rusted bolts scraping securely into place and he knew that he was now a prisoner in the Castle of the Bears.

In the room there was a low wooden bed, piled high at one end with a collection of dull grey coarse woven blankets. Next to the bed stood a stool on which sat a thick candle sweating gobbets of wax onto a silver plate and casting a warm yellow light over a bowl of steaming hot stew. On the floor, half under the stool and mostly hidden in shadow, squatted a stout earthenware pitcher of water.

The good knight did not sleep well. The bed was hard and uncomfortable and he could find no warmth between the woven blankets that merely caused him to scratch at an ever elusive itch. No matter which way he turned he could feel an icy draught on his face, nipping his nose and burning his cheeks. Once the candle burned itself out the good knight might have despaired had it not been for the thin yellow ribbon of light that filtered through from the passageway outside his room and marked the bottom edge of the door. He lay shivering and awake, watching this faint beacon until the early morning brought the bears back to his cell.

On hearing the thump thump of the bears' footsteps as they padded along the corridor to his room, the good knight threw off the blankets and sat up on the edge of the bed boards ready for their entrance. The bolts jerked complainingly back and the door was pushed open filling the room with the broken light from the still smoking lanterns that hung outside. The shadows of the two bears fell tall and featureless across the floor of the cell and the good knight got to his feet. His arms clamped to his sides again, he was march back along the twisting corridors, not to the grand hall as he expected, but straight to the main entrance to the castle.

The inner door was closed and in front of it a small group of bears headed by the great black bear were assembled to send the good knight on his way. The black bear, dressed in a long flowing cape the colour of dried blood and edged with a decorative fringe of gold coins that clinked together whenever it moved, greeted the good knight with an unpleasant growl.

'Remember, I want that fish for my supper tonight!' barked the bear and it handed the good knight the reins of a simple wooden sled on which a dirty cloth parcel had been secured. The inner door swung open and the good knight was pushed into the dark

47

passageway towards the great oak outer door. The chains, operated by invisible claws, jangled loosely and the heavy door ground painfully open. The good knight, without looking back, left the Castle of the Bears and with it his great white horse and all that he possessed in the world. Dragging the sled at his heels, he headed off across the snow, off and away to the distant hills.

The snow had stopped sometime during the night and with it the wind had died so that the good knight's trek to the hill that resembled a crouching lion was not as long nor as arduous as it might have been. The climb up the hill, too, was a good deal easier than he had expected, burdened as he was with the wooden sled. The sun was not even at its height when he stood staring down into the still black water of the pool that lay in the dip between the lion's shoulders. He knelt over the sled and untied the leather straps that fixed the cloth parcel to the wooden base. Inside the stained cloth wrapping there was a large net weighted at intervals with smooth shiny black rocks each the size of a clenched fist, and a smaller parcel that contained some scraps of bread and a small ceramic jar with a piece of wood jammed in at its neck. The good knight was not sure if the bread was meant for him, or if it was included so that he might entice the fish to the surface of the water, but his journey to this black pool had so sapped his energies that before thinking the good knight had eaten the best part of the scraps of bread. He could not extract the wooden plug from the jar so he dipped his hands into the black pool and scooped up a mouthful of the coldest, clearest water he had ever seen or tasted. Then, refreshed and eager, he set about casting the net clumsily out over the water.

Each time that the good knight pulled the empty net back in, his face fell and his spirits sank. He quietly untangled the net and spread it flat on the snow like a thick dark spider's web circled by the shiny hard bloated bodies of a dozen spiders waiting to pounce on anything that fell into the mesh of knotted cords. Then again he spun the net above his head and cast it out into the water with a wild splash that lapped at the far shore of the pool. He watched it sink out of sight and waited for the bubbles to finish popping at the surface before beginning the slow haul back, hopeful this time that his efforts would be rewarded.

After a while the good knight began to tire, each cast of the net falling nearer and nearer the shore where he stood until he could hardly lift his arms, and his hands – cut and bleeding from hauling the net – were frozen from the cold water of the pool. He could no longer grip the net sufficiently firmly to drag it back in and so he let the sodden cord slide through his fingers as he fell to his knees on the cold wet ground. His hands rested palms up on his knees, like the half-clenched claws of a dead bird. His shoulders slumped and his head hung down so that his chin touched his chest and with each desperate breath rose and fell in a slow sad nod.

Suddenly there was a splash in the centre of the pool and the good knight looked up in time to see a glittering silver tail disappearing back beneath the broken glassy surface of the water. He watched and waited, not daring to believe what his eyes had just seen. The ripples fanned out evenly from the middle of the pool, and then flattened so that it quickly regained its flat mirror-like quality. He got to his feet and shouted after the fish.

'Wait, come back!'

His words, the first he had uttered since leaving the Castle of the Bears, returned to him in an indistinct echo. But the fish did not reappear. He picked up the cord that was attached to the empty net and started to pull it in. The fleeting sight of the fish had lifted his spirits and the tiredness he had felt only a moment before left him. He hauled the net out of the water and prepared it as before. Then with an effort of will he threw the net far into the middle of the pool, just where he had seen the fish tail slip below the surface. He waited for the net to sink and then he began to pull on the cord. This time the net was heavy and strained his whole body with each pull as he bent and straightened by turns, drawing it inch by inch nearer to the shallows at the edge of the pool. And as it reached the surface of the water the good knight could see his own reflection in the shiny silver scales of the great fish caught in the tight mesh.

The more certain it became that he would land the fish, the more earnestly the fish thrashed its body against the knotted cords of the net and with its tail flicked icy cold showers of water spraying down over the good knight. Even when the great fish had been dragged out of the shallows and lay beyond help in the snow at the feet of the good knight, it continued to toss its head and twist its body in a desperate bid to free itself and return to the water. The fish was indeed a great fish. Lying there on the ground, the good knight could see that from nose to tail it was as long as he was tall and at its thickest point almost as broad. He bent to pick up some of the scales that had rubbed off in the fish's energetic struggle. They were like blank silver coins in the cupped palm of his hand, glistening with a delicate iridescent sheen that moved whenever he tried to touch it. He scooped up some more out of the snow and, not understanding why, except that their beauty so fascinated him, he pushed them into the pocket of his breeches.

The good knight knelt to unwrap the net from the great fish, but as soon as his hand touched the slippery silver body it stopped its agitated threshing, turned its head to the good knight and spoke to him in a quiet, clear voice. It was not that the fish spoke that the good knight found remarkable, it was what the fish said that startled him and made him jerk his hands back from its body as if burned by fire and he tumbled backwards into the snow.

'Do not think that the black bear won't eat you, too, good knight,' said the fish.

The good knight scrambled to a crouching position on all fours and looked at the fish in alarm. The fish reiterated its warning in the same clear voice.

'Do not think that I will be the only supper dish in the Castle of the Bears tonight.'

'But we have an agreement,' said the good knight defensively, though his confidence in the agreement was already evaporating.

'If we help each other, good knight, then we can both live. It is the only way. I can return to my pool and you can ride away from the Castle of the Bears on your great white horse,' said the fish still staring at the good knight with its wet unblinking eye that shone like a ring of liquid gold.

Uncertainty and distrust showed on the good knight's face. He remained crouched and facing the great fish, the muscles in his arms and legs tensed ready for flight.

'You have no reason to fear me, good knight, am I not your prisoner?' said the great fish confidently. 'Please unwind this net from me and we can discuss the plan for your escape.'

Without a word the good knight approached the great fish and hesitantly began unpicking the tangled web from its cold slippery body. He worked slowly and with care, anxious now not to tear the transparently thin spiky feathered fins that snagged on the net's cords. A frozen numbness had returned to his fingers making his task more than doubly difficult. The cold water flicked over him in the great fish's efforts to resist capture had soaked through his clothes to his skin and a juddering shiver gradually overcame the good knight.

When he finally unravelled the puzzle, combed out the last knot and peeled back the last binding strands of the net, the great fish arched its body and with a single dramatic thrust propelled itself through the air to land back in the pool. It snaked its body through the shallows leaving a foaming trail in its wake and quickly disappeared into the deeper darker water.

The good knight looked on in disbelief, too cold to obstruct the great fish's getaway. But before disbelief could turn to despair the fish was back at the surface of the pool. It twisted through the shallows again and came to rest near the shore. From there it began to explain to the good knight all that he was to do and how the plan would unfold. The good knight listened, nodding all the time, never doubting but that what the fish said must be true. He asked no questions when the fish finished speaking, so it flipped round, returned to the deep water and swam off without another word. It all happened so quickly that the good knight forgot to thank the great fish. 'How can I ever repay you?' he shouted.

The fish gave no answer but leaped out of the water in a wide arc, the water dripping from its silver scales and catching the sun's bright rays to form a gossamer thin rainbow that was there and gone in the blink of the good knight's eyes.

The good knight wrapped up the net in the stained cloth and tied it to the sled and, following the fish's instructions, he began his return journey to the Castle of the Bears. He took the same path down that he had taken up, lowering the sled first until it rested on some narrow ledge or against an obstinate boulder, then slipping and sliding his way to land level with the sled again. Each time he came to rest he turned and looked towards the Castle of the Bears, for even at this distance he could feel their staring eyes fixed on him.

At the base of the hill there was a small hollow in the land where the good knight disappeared from view for a moment. Here, precisely as the fish had described it, was a large smooth oval-shaped rock. To avoid suspicion the good knight had to move quickly.

He pulled the cloth parcel off of the sled and tossed the net to one side. He threw the cloth over one shoulder and dragged the sled alongside the rock. He bent his knees and hugged the rock with outstretched arms. Then, bracing himself, he tightened his hold and pushed up with his legs. The rock was not quite as large as the great fish, but it was a deal heavier and the effort needed to shift it was considerable, but the good knight managed to lift it onto the sled. It creaked under the weight. He took the cloth and draped it over the oval rock and bound it tightly to the sled. The whole operation took barely two minutes from the moment the good knight disappeared from sight to the moment he reappeared hauling the loaded sled behind him.

His progress back to the Castle of the Bears was slow and hard. Where before the sled had slid easily across the surface of the snow, now, under the weight of the oval rock, its runners dug deep and the good knight, with the reins strapped to his waist, had to use both arms to pull the sled forward.

The sun sank lower in the sky and the air became chill and sharp, but the good knight did not lose heart. It was all going according to the great fish's plan. Every few steps he stopped to catch his breath and to pick up out of the snow a thick stick or blunt gnarled branch of a long-dead tree, the thinly scattered remains of a forest that had grown there in a time before the Castle of the Bears. He wedged each piece of wood onto the sled, jammed between the rock and the wooden base, twisted over the rock and woven in and out of the other branches so that very soon he had gathered a collection of wood that formed a spiky dome over the rock, like some huge unkempt hedgehog.

When the good knight was still some way off from the castle he looked up at the sky. It was a blackish blue with a trail of red-streaked clouds floating towards the setting sun. He could see the castle only as a shadowy, ill-defined blackness and knew then that the darkness now shielded him from the bears' scrutiny. He pulled the sled to a halt and began to unload the wood, piling it into a small mound. Again he worked quickly. He pulled the sled and the oval rock off to the right of the pile of wood and covered it in snow so that it appeared as nothing more than an unevenness in the landscape. He carefully wiped away his tracks and retreated to the woodpile. Then he headed off empty handed towards the grand entrance to the Castle of the Bears.

He knocked three times with the ball of his clenched fist on the huge oak door and two flaming torches materialised on the top of the two towers that stood either side of the entrance. By the orange light that they cast as the bears above peered down at him he could see that the giant carved knights-at-arms that flanked the great doorway were in fact broad-snouted bears-at-arms, their oversized heads glowering menacingly down at him. The good knight looked back to the door in front of him.

Up above, the torches vanished as the two guards hurried away to open the great door. The clanking chain and the screaming of wood against stone was followed by silence.

This time the good knight would not enter into the blind tunnel that led to the second inner door. He stepped back from the outer door and waited. He could hear the confused grunting of the guards inside, then the deeper more resonant and commanding growl of the big black bear. Suddenly the passageway beyond was filled with brightness and heavy movement and the good knight felt his heart race as he prepared to confront the bears.

It was no real surprise that the black bear, still dressed in its flowing gown fringed with jingling gold coins, was the first to leap out from behind the great oak door.

'Well, simple knight, where is my supper?' it barked gruffly.

An armed group of bears, swords drawn and flaming torches raised above their heads, formed a threatening line behind the big black bear.

The good knight breathed deeply and opened his mouth to deliver the speech he had been mentally rehearsing since hiding the sled with the oval rock in the snow.

'How do I know you will keep your end of the bargain?' he began. 'You could just as easily have me, my horse and the fish for your supper this evening. How can you guarantee that you will set me and my horse free?'

The black bear staggered one step backwards, stumbling into the arms of the bears behind. Two torches fell hissing angrily into the snow and were extinguished in a cloud of steam.

'Bring me a large shallow basin and I will cook your fish out here,' said the good knight, not letting the black bear recover enough to start talking. 'Then, when the fish is ready, you can come alone with my horse and we can do a swap.'

The great black bear advanced on the good knight. 'You dare to dictate terms to me? Why, I could crush you dead with one blow, you little man.'

'And then you would not find your fish until the snow melts, by which time it would be nothing more than a rotting carcass,' said the good knight standing his ground.

'How do I know you even have the fish?' said the great black bear, straightening up until it looked down on the good knight from a great height.

'How do I know you still have my horse and all my possessions?' parried the good knight.

The black bear turned to the bears at its back and grunted loudly, waving one of them back into the castle with a violent jerk of one of its thick paws. The bear returned after only a brief interlude leading the good knight's great white horse by a tightly grasped rein.

'There you are!' said the black bear. 'Now where's the fish?'

The good knight would not be tricked into showing the great black bear the fish. He reached his hand into the pocket of his breeches and brought out some of the smooth round silver scales he had collected from the snow beside the black pool. He held out his hand for the black bear to see the shiny 'coins' shimmering in the torchlight. The bear lowered its head and sniffed at the scales in the good knight's hand. Then it turned and, pushing through the line of bears behind, marched back into the castle grunting gruffly to itself. The other bears lowered their swords and followed on after the great black bear, the last one leading the great white horse meekly in through the castle door.

Left alone the good knight had time to reflect on what had just happened. The great black bear could indeed have crushed the life from him with one blow and yet he had dared to face up to it. He had not even flinched when the bear had towered angrily over him.

He knew the fish had given him the confidence to do that. However, the memory of it now made his knees weak and a cool sweat dampened his brow.

He started as heavy footsteps padded to the still open dark oak door. This time it was only one of the guard bears carrying the large shallow basin which he had requested. He sensed a new respect in the bear's deferential manner and when the bear laid the basin at his feet his confidence vaulted over his good sense and he heard himself asking for a torch too. The bear retreated into the passageway without turning its back on the good knight and returned with a yellow flaming torch which it stuck in the ground beside the basin. The good knight thanked the bear with a grin and watched it back off into the castle again. The chains clanked noisily and the oak door ground slowly shut.

He snatched up the torch in one hand and with the other tried to lift the shallow basin. Its shape and size made this impossible so, taking hold of the thick rim, he lugged it behind him as best he could manage and, by the light of the torch, retraced his footsteps in the snow to the pile of wood. There he collected four flat-topped rocks and arranged them around the wood making a firm base to balance the basin on. Then, though the snow froze his fingers, he shovelled handfuls into the basin until it was full and heaped high.

From underneath his jerkin he drew out the small ceramic jar that had been hidden in the cloth parcel and which he had been unable to open because of the piece of wood jammed in at its neck. He broke its neck on the rim of the basin and emptied its contents into the snow he had collected. The jar contained a thick syrupy wine and would help to create a rich stock with a strong sweet aroma.

He was ready. Let the black bear come now, he thought with some satisfaction. He stuffed the burning torch into the wood and watched the flames lick blue-tongued up the sides of the basin. He heard the old wood crack and split and the snow in the basin begin to hiss.

Just as he was about to call for the black bear to bring out his great white horse he let out a loud gasp of shock as if he had been slapped hard across his face. He had forgotten the vital ingredient, the oval rock still strapped to the sled and buried in the snow. If he could forget this most important element then there was still a chance that things could go very wrong. He must stay on his guard a little longer yet.

He ran to where he had buried the sled and getting behind it he pushed it up to the fire. He unwound the leather cord that secured the rock to the base of the sled, but made sure that the rock remained covered by the stained cloth. The snow in the basin had melted by this time and it was full to the brim with a cloudy sweet smelling stock, just as the fish had guessed it would be, and small bubbles were beginning to break on the surface. Now he really was ready. The good knight cupped his hands to his mouth and called to the great black bear waiting in the castle.

'Bring forth my great white horse for your supper is prepared!'

Perhaps it sounded a bit formal. He hoped that it did not hint at the trickery that was to follow. He tried to focus his thoughts on everything that the fish had told him. He folded his arms across his chest and steadied his breathing. It would not do to pick up the oval rock too soon, he decided, so the good knight stood, feet apart, with the fire between him and the castle and his eyes straining for some sign that the bear was approaching.

The castle door opened with that grinding screech that was becoming familiar to the good knight, and by the light that spilled out onto the snow he saw the great black bear pulling his great white horse with one paw and the other holding aloft a fresh torch dripping stringy trails of flaming pitch. The castle door closed again and the good knight watched the black bear move easily across the snow towards the steaming basin. Its flowing red cloak dragged in the snow, but every few steps the good knight caught the faint jingling sound of the coins fastened to the hem.

Ten steps before reaching the basin the black bear stopped and craned its snout forward, sniffing the air. Could it smell treachery, the good knight wondered. He let his arms fall to his sides and, hoping that the black bear could not see, wiped his sweating palms on his breeches. The sweet smell of the good knight's cooking and the thought of cooked fish made the black bear's mouth water and it bounced up to the basin in three long leaps.

'Smells good, simple knight,' said the black bear, dribbling spit from its eager mouth.

'It's just the stock. I have yet to add the fish,' said the good knight truthfully. 'Let go the reins of my horse and then you can have your supper.'

The black bear did as he was commanded and the good knight click clacked with his tongue on the roof of his mouth. The great white horse shied away from the great black bear and paced to the good knight, nuzzling him in the small of his back with his nose.

'Now the fish!' demanded the great black bear.

'Now the fish,' said the good knight bending to the oval rock on the sled.

What happened next happened very quickly but with all the unreality of a dream. The black bear moved closer to the basin sniffing the air all the while. The good knight lifted the oval rock, being careful to keep the cloth in place. They faced each other, eyes meeting across the bubbling stock for one fleeting moment. Then the good knight heaved the rock forward into the basin with all the force that he could muster. The great rock crashed into the soup with a mighty splash sending boiling stock flying into the face of the great black bear. The good knight grabbed at the reins of his great white horse just as the black bear let drop its torch and all light was extinguished in an instant.

The darkness all around reverberated with an agonised roaring that mixed anger and pain in equal amount. The good knight felt his way into the saddle of his great white horse and urged it to fly like the wind away from the black bear and the Castle of the Bears. And that's just what the great white horse did.

The fierce roaring of the black bear followed at their heels, but they kept going without looking back and the great black bear, blinded by the boiling broth, could not pursue them.

Before the bears in the castle had plucked up the courage to venture out from the safety of the high walls to discover what had happened to cause such terrible screams, the good knight and his great white horse had escaped to the far away hills. There in a still black pool a silver tailed fish leapt free of the icy water and drew a perfect silver arc in the air before disappearing back into the black liquid.

Dragon Slayer by Nikola Temkov

I have a Daughter

by Catherine Edmunds

"I have a daughter."

My father's deep tones rang out, commanding silence, and the moment I'd been dreading since I turned sixteen finally arrived. I clutched Shull's fur and watched intently from behind the grill that had helped keep me invisible all these years.

The tall warrior's eyes lit up. These were the first words of a ritual, and barbarian or no, he knew them well, but had never expected to hear them himself. None in the hall would have known of my existence; the fact that my father had a daughter. There was a murmuring of surprise, then a hushing to silence.

"I have a daughter," my father repeated, softly this time, and this time the warrior responded. The ritualistic words were spoken harshly, his voice cracking with the strain of sudden unexpected hope.

"I have need of a wife."

There were more whispers. This warrior had come to my father's aid when no others would or could; he had enabled victory when all hope was lost; he deserved reward – of course he did. But he was a barbarian. An outsider. My father had gold in abundance. A barbarian should have been satisfied. Perhaps my father saw some quality in this stranger, beyond mere prowess in arms that the rest of us didn't.

I shuddered. I didn't want my existence to be made public. I didn't want the barbarian's rough hands touching me. I wanted to stay hidden; cared for by Shull and my mother (well, maybe I could do without Mother) in the dark garden within the castle keep. I was safe there; nobody could break through the thorns that protected me. My few forays out were along secret passages to hidden viewing points, such as this one that allowed me to follow the goings-on in the Great Hall. I had hoped to live all my life this way; safe, secure, hidden. And now? Now I was to be given to this stranger. Offered up to a barbarian to wed and bed. That meant babies. And babies meant heartache. Boy children were safe enough, but girls were not. Few reached adulthood before they disappeared. Anxious parents kept them hidden away, protected by incantations and spells and the more practical means of the wolf-like race of protectors; Shull and his kindred. Yet still they disappeared, and a full grown girl-child was a rarity. Women thus had become highly prized. But instead of giving us power, it made us bargaining tools; objects of ritual; possessions which were less than human.

I looked back into the Great Hall. The barbarian warrior was kneeling before my father. Jobert, the wizard, had materialised from somewhere and was doing something clever with smoke; sending it first around my father's neck before snaking it out to the barbarian to bind them together forever. I was fascinated, despite my revulsion. The wizard raised his head and stared straight at me through the grill. He wasn't supposed to know I even existed, but of course he'd always known. He sent a small, private smile of encouragement to me, and then continued officiating over the ceremony.

I couldn't watch any more. I sat down on the floor and held Shull close, burying my face in his fur. He nipped me playfully on the ear, reminding me of the puppy he'd once been; my playmate as a child – my protector ever since. I suddenly wanted to marry Shull. Daft idea, I knew, as you can't marry a wolf, but still...

"*What* do you think you're doing with that animal?" asked my mother, as she came hurrying through the door with her entourage of black wolves. They snarled and snapped at Shull, who took no notice. Mother must have been angry to have set them off like that. They'd been with her so long that her consciousness and theirs had thoroughly melded. They made her emotions blindingly obvious by their demeanour. That annoyed Mother, which in turn made her companions even snappier, but it was useful from my point of view.

"What am I doing? I'm hugging Shull, my one true love. What does it look like I'm doing?"

Shull hiccupped, trying to suppress the giggles that I was feeling.

Mother sat down on the floor next to me and unexpectedly burst into tears.

"Mum? You all right?"

"Oh my daughter... my daughter... he's given you away. How could he? To a savage! I'll be alone now. All, all alone."

I thought of giving her a hug, but I'd never done it before and didn't feel like starting now. Her wolves were howling, and Shull buried his muzzle in my armpit, making me giggle again – a most inappropriate reaction. He was right though. After my initial shock at being bargained away to some rough barbarian, I was starting to feel elated. I'd be escaping Mother and her fat tears; I'd have my own 'establishment', and, scary but possible, I might even get to go outside. Mother never ventured out, but that was her choice. She would have been safe enough, now her child bearing years were over.

I looked through the grill at the barbarian again. The ritual was over and everyone was drinking beer and celebrating. My father and his future son-in-law were clearly going to get very drunk together tonight. I wanted to join in, but no, it wasn't possible. Not yet. Not until after the wedding.

Would the tall handsome barbarian with the cold eyes and rough voice even like me? Father didn't much like Mother, but it had never mattered. She was safe and grateful; and he had a wife, which meant sons to carry on his bloodline, and a daughter for bargaining purposes.

Mother wiped her tears away, stopped sniffling, and managed to look purposeful.

"You'll have to learn the ways of men now. I'd better start instructing you."

"No thanks, Mum."

"But you have to know."

"Shull can tell me."

"Shull's a wolf, not a man, dammit. He's an animal – he can't tell you anything."

I laid a calming hand on Shull's head.

"He can tell me all I need to know."

Mother gave me a withering look, got up off the floor, dusted down her gown, and bustled away down the corridor, duty done. I was relieved. I hadn't wanted some great lecture about the evils of men's nasty ways. I'd learn all of that soon enough.

I turned back to look into the Great Hall. The barbarian and my father were singing. Badly. Did I really have to marry this hulking fool? Jobert glanced up, as if catching my thoughts. Yes, I did, his look said.

*

My wedding day was my first foray into 'company'. I walked down the aisle on my father's arm, heavily veiled, but feeling more vulnerable than ever. The entire household was in the Great Hall to watch; all these people that I knew so well from observing them over the years, but who hadn't even known of my existence until a few weeks ago.

Shull walked behind me, forever faithful. Jobert stood ahead, waiting to officiate, a kindly smile on his face encouraging me as ever. The barbarian – I didn't even know his name yet – stood patiently, head to the front, hands twitching slightly. Nerves? I hoped so.

A few minutes later, the tall stranger – who I now learnt was called Bolor, a pretty ghastly name – lifted the veil from my head, kissed me decorously, and we were wed. I was safe. I wouldn't disappear.

My husband turned to my father and spoke.

"I have adhered to your customs and wed the daughter of this house. Now you must adhere to mine."

With that, this tall warrior, honoured guest in our home and saviour of my father's kingdom, unsheathed his sword and with one sweep, decapitated Shull. My beloved wolf's blood poured out from his severed neck and spurted onto my wedding gown. I shrieked and attacked the assassin with my bare fists, grazing and bruising my knuckles but doing him no harm whatsoever.

"No!" shouted my father; but to me, not to the murderer to whom I was now tied forever. Rough hands pulled me away from Bolor, but not before I'd landed a hard kick on his shin, cracking two of my toes as a result. I was led – or dragged, rather – to my chamber where I flung myself onto my bed and wept with anguish for my dead love. I was mercifully left alone, and finally cried myself to sleep.

When I awoke, Mother was fussing over me. I remembered her words from a few weeks ago: "You'll have to learn the ways of men now. I'd better start instructing you," and the way I'd dismissed them, arrogantly assuming there was nothing she could tell me of any use.

"Why, Mum? Why did he kill Shull?"

"I don't know. Jealousy, I should imagine. He saw the way Shull was guarding you. He considers that his duty now – which it is, of course. But still. I'm sorry it happened that way. I know you were fond of the wolf. Too fond, if you ask me. It wasn't natural, you know."

Mother always did that. Said something nice, and then spoilt it. She frowned at me.

"Look, I know you don't want to listen to me. No reason why you should. But listen to Jobert. I'm sure he can explain all this better than I can. Rituals and things. I don't pretend to understand them. He has books. He can even read them. He's wise."

She flapped and fussed, but I turned away. Mother was right; I didn't want to listen to her. I didn't even want Jobert and his books at the moment. I wanted Shull. I wanted his hard furry body next to mine. I wanted him snuffling up and looking at me with his great gentle eyes. I wanted... my love. I didn't want his murderer. Could I run away? Escape? Raise an army, come back and seek revenge? What a hope. Of course I couldn't.

The one sensible piece of advice she'd given me was to listen to Jobert, though he would no doubt tell me to be a good little girl and honour and obey my lord and master. Was I to be locked into this vile marriage for the rest of my life, slowly souring, just as my mother had done? That was a thought. Had something similar happened to her? Was that the problem? No, probably not. She was just a stupid woman, who didn't know when she was well off. She'd survived; she'd borne children; she'd kept her daughter. It was rare. She didn't deserve such good fortune.

Shull would have nipped me on the heels for such an uncharitable thought. Shull... suddenly I was crying again, great sobs wracking my body. Mother tut-tutted in that annoying way she has, and left me to it.

63

An hour or so later, I became aware of a faint aroma of incense in the air. Jobert had come in and was standing by the window. I watched his elegant profile with the hooked nose, lined cheeks and pewter hair that glinted copper in the evening sun. The colour was strange. Was it caused by magic? Or hair dye? It was a strange thought to have at such a time. My head felt woozy. Jobert must have burned something to make me sleep, to give me time to recover.

He turned, and knelt before me.

"My lady."

The wizard and I had never spoken to each other before, other than the words of ritual during the wedding ceremony, but I knew what to say. I'd seen Mother do this.

"Arise, Jobert. I am pleased. Now speak." Formalities over, I relaxed. "Oh, and call me Krissa."

He smiled. I'd said the right thing.

"Krissa, I'm so sorry about Shull. I would have warned you if I'd known. I wondered afterwards if your mother might have done, but," he looked at his feet in their surprisingly prosaic laced up boots; "it seems she didn't."

"No. She didn't."

My eyes followed his to his feet, but then jumped up again and I stared with concentration at the top of his head. He'd done his laces up wrongly. If I looked at his feet, I might start giggling hysterically. I was in a strange mood.

"Bolor is a good man, Krissa, but he is as bound by his own traditions, as are we by ours. However, there is more to this man than meets the eye. I've spoken to him and tried to understand. He says he didn't kill Shull."

I forgot about the wizard's feet, and listened closely to his words. He looked out of the window and continued in a quiet voice.

"I don't understand this. He admits to the decapitation, but laughs at the idea of death. Perhaps it's some theory of the afterlife. I can't tell – this is beyond me."

Jobert looked back at me nervously and changed the subject.

"You know, I can give you something – a strengthening potion, to help you through this."

"Through what?"

"The, well, errm… the begetting of children."

"Oh, that."

The actual begetting was the least of my worries. What followed mattered far more.

"Jobert, what happens to the girl babies? Why do so few of us survive?"

"I really don't know. I wish we had enough wolves for protection, as they seem to be the only effective solution, but alas, they rarely breed, and their numbers are declining. I can only advise you to guard any female progeny well, my dear."

"But have you no theories?"

"Oh yes. I have read the histories. Dragons were undoubtedly the original culprits."

"But there are no such creatures as dragons. Not any more."

"Oh, not literal ones. Or maybe. I don't know. Yes, all the real dragons were killed centuries ago, but, hmm… I'm going to have to ask Bolor about this, I think."

"Bolor? Why would he know any more? He's not from dragon country."

"No, but going back to what he did, or didn't do to your wolf – if he thinks Shull isn't really dead, then maybe he has some theory about the dragons not being really dead either. We might think the Sameerdoie killed them all, but I don't know. Did they? They're a strange people."

"In what way?"

"Scaly. Dragonish."

I frowned. I knew what he meant. I'd seen a few of the Sameerdoie at festivals, where they were honoured for the age-old service of destroying the ravening beasts, and though they'd never struck me as particularly dragonish – no fire breathing, or anything like that – they did keep their eyes covered with silken visors. I'd always assumed that was due to some sensitivity to light, or a tradition of modesty. Maybe it was to hide the double eyelids. Did they have forked tongues too? Carefully folded wings under the heavy armour? No, the idea was absurd. Laughable.

"Good to see you smile, little one."

"Little?"

"I've been quietly overseeing your care since you were tiny. Still think of you as little."

"My father doesn't know that, I bet."

He chuckled.

"No, certainly not. But your father isn't a wizard. I have certain advantages when it comes to knowing what's going on. Talking of which, your husband's approaching. Be kind to him Krissa. He's a good man. Don't make any hasty judgements."

With that, he bowed, smiled, and drifted out of the room.

I stood up, straightened my gown, and prepared to meet the arrogant stranger who thought it mattered not one jot that he had killed his wife's only true love on her wedding day.

Bolor walked in and smiled at me with Shull's eyes and I came close to passing out with desire.

"Shull?" I gasped.

"No, Bolor. But I'm glad you can see Shull in me. Didn't really want another kick... Come here."

He held out his arms, and I walked into them gladly. He nuzzled my neck, and it was Shull's breath I felt. I shuddered with relief. Everything was going to be all right. I was not going to end up old and sour like my mother. I was not going to have to raise armies to defeat my husband. I might even fall in love with him.

*

Five years passed. I bore one son and twin daughters. My son grew strong and thrived; but his sisters had gone; had disappeared, just before their third birthday. My heart had come close to breaking. The pain was well nigh unbearable. They had been guarded so closely; kept in the castle grounds forever under the eye of a multitude of guards. Instead of being locked in a dark garden as I'd been, we'd given them the run of the castle in order to make them strong and brave, so that everyone would see and rejoice in them and grow to love them. Secrecy was not the answer, Bolor and I agreed. They needed to be guarded by everyone; not just a few thorn bushes, a wolf and a wizard who couldn't even tie his shoe laces properly.

It should have worked. We had a whole pack of wolves, and each child had a personal guard of Sameerdoie, the brave race who'd been responsible for ridding the land of the scourge of dragons.

How could it have happened? I was interviewing Grolland, the Captain of the Sameerdoie, yet again, fearful that the next child I carried would be another daughter. I longed for daughters, but didn't think I could bear further loss.

"Lady, I do not know. We watch. We sniff. We taste the air. We wait. Yet we see nothing."

"I know, I know; I'm not accusing you of negligence, Grolland. I'm just trying to understand."

He put a scaly hand out to comfort me, then appeared embarrassed and withdrew it quickly. He coughed, and I was sure I smelled smoke. People joked about the Sameerdoie turning into dragons, but this was something Bolor and I had looked into very carefully before engaging them as guards. He was of the opinion that having slain the dragons, they had undoubtedly taken on dragon characteristics – just as Bolor had become Shull, absorbing the essence of my beloved wolf even as he beheaded him. So yes, the dragons lived on through the Sameerdoie. They had absorbed dragonish strength and resilience. The side effect of scaly skin and the occasional fire breathing had turned them into a race that many feared, but we were convinced they were not evil in any way, and were in fact the most effective of guards.

Grolland coughed again.

"Lady, they are magicked away. That is the only explanation. We guard. The wolves guard. None could do better. Ask your wizard. Therein lies the lack. I'm sorry Lady. Where is the strength of wizards? Ask Jobert."

"Jobert guarded me well when I was young."

Grolland shrugged.

"Even so."

"Not Jobert."

I shook my head.

Grolland shrugged again, bowed stiffly, and took his leave.

I closed my eyes, rested back on the chair, and let my thoughts wander. I was tired, and so, so sad about my daughters. Jobert, carrying off little girls all over the land? It was hardly likely. When I was in this state, I would often imagine sweet nymph-like creatures, elven maidens, coming to me and telling me not to worry; my daughters were safe, they were in the country of Yspereth, an elven land where none could harm them. It was a comforting thought, but it was not enough. I needed to know where they really went; who stole them away.

I'd invented Yspereth when I was little. As soon as I'd learned to hold a quill and dip it in ink without making too much mess, I'd started drawing pictures of the magical kingdom where elves danced with children and sang and spun wonderful tales full of magic and kindness and laughter. Mother couldn't teach me to write, as she didn't know how, but she was happy enough for me to draw, as it kept me from under her feet.

My invented land was so different to my real dark existence with its brief glimpses into my father's world through narrow hidden grills, and the mundane world of laundry and cooking that my mother inhabited. I longed for Yspereth and wanted to go there so badly.

I used to wander round my dark garden beneath the massy castle, hunting for a magic key that would lead me to the magical land. One day I would find the key, I was sure. But I was so closely guarded I never did, and the childish dreams faded, only returning when I was particularly unhappy and needing solace.

I'd never told Shull about Yspereth and the elven maidens. Never told Bolor, either. He wouldn't have understood. He didn't have a need for light, the way I did, having grown up in a land where he could run and shoot and ride in the open to his heart's content.

I fell asleep dreaming of nymphs riding golden dragons who breathed fire that lit up the sky without burning. When I awoke, there were tears on my cheeks, and such longing. Were there really no more dragons? Had the Sameerdoie killed them all? Were they really evil? Or was that just received wisdom; an assumption.

No, it had to be true. I remembered one night in the Great Hall, hidden behind my grill, when I'd listened to a troubadour singing of a mountain, many hundreds of miles away that had been their last refuge. It had breathed fire and laid vast areas to waste, until finally all the dragons had been killed and the mountain could sleep.

Bolor found me in a wistful mood when he came in later.
"What's up, love?"
"Dreams."

"About what?"

"Oh, you know. Dragons and nymphs and elves and magic and... daughters."

"Ah love, I'm sorry."

He sat down beside me and put his arms around me, rocking me gently.

"Bolor, were dragons really so dangerous?"

"Yes, no question. We have the written evidence of those who lived through such times. It's depressing stuff. I must teach you to read," he added, thoughtfully.

"Oh yes love, do, please. We have books full of squiggles – I can't imagine that they're really words. I'd love to be able to read them. I asked Jobert, but he laughed. Said women had the wrong sort of brain; couldn't make the right connections to make sense of written language. I didn't believe him."

"Quite right. I know it's not the done thing, but if you want to read, no reason why you shouldn't."

"So what did the books say about dragons?"

"That they carried off more than just sheep. No child was safe; especially not girl children."

"Why did they go for girls?"

Bolor looked embarrassed.

"Maybe because girls couldn't escape so easily."

"Why not? They can run as fast as boys, I'd have thought?"

"Probably, though their elaborate clothing might have hindered them. But the point is; the boys had their ponies. Girls didn't."

"What? Why not?"

"Girls were raised to be homemakers, not to fight or hunt. What need would they have for riding skills?"

"Oh, you're joking, surely."

"No, love. It's how it was. How it had always been."

"But why didn't people start teaching the girls to ride too, to safeguard them?"

"It was seen as improper. The better solution was to get rid of the dragons. That way the girls could stay pretty and feminine, and the problem would be solved."

69

I wanted to kick Bolor in the shins again, but desisted, due to memories of cracked toes.

"They wanted to keep the girls as drudges; as slaves, in other words."

"I wouldn't put it quite so strongly, but yes, I suppose so. There was a fear of strength in women; of independent thought and action. So it was far better to remove the danger and safeguard them that way."

"But it's backfired, hasn't it."

"Yes, and nobody really knows why. The dragons were destroyed. The girls should have been safe. But they still continued to disappear." Bolor looked thoughtful. "You know, sometimes I think the dragons weren't to blame for even the sheep; not really. I know they took them, but you don't blame an owl for eating a mouse, after all. It's the natural order of things. Dragons eat sheep, so it's up to men to keep their sheep safe. And I'm not even sure about the children. The girls."

"How do you mean?"

"I don't know why dragons would want to eat girls, when sheep were so plentiful. What if the historians decided to blame the dragons for the girls' disappearance because the real truth was too shameful? Why did certain merchants, for example, grow rich back then, without having obviously earned their wealth or captured it in battle? Traders, who were dealing in a small way in woollen textiles, would suddenly build themselves grand castles. Were they trading in more than just wool? You blame your ancestors for treating girls as slaves, but there are worse kinds of slavery. I wonder what those merchants were trading in... they certainly made plenty of money; easily enough to bribe historians to blame the dragons."

It was a horribly believable theory, especially as I wanted – really wanted – the dragons not to be to blame. I trusted Grolland. He had some dragon blood, it was clear, yet he was obviously trustworthy. But did he feel guilt? Were the silken visors of the Sameerdoie there to cover the guilt in their eyes? The knowledge that they had destroyed a race that had done no evil?

"That could explain the stolen children from the time of the dragons. But what about now? Why do girls still disappear? Where are my daughters? They were too closely guarded to have been simply been stolen away by traders. You know that. How could it have happened, Bolor?"

"I don't know, love. I just don't know."

"Grolland says they were 'magicked' away and that I should question Jobert."

"Question a wizard who successfully guarded you throughout your childhood, and raised you to be the darling woman I see before me now? Doesn't sound like a very good idea, my love. Your very presence is evidence of his trustworthiness. No, I don't think Jobert knows any more than we do. In fact, I'd say he's deeply frustrated by his ignorance. I've often seen him pacing to and fro along the battlements arguing with himself and trying to find solutions."

"And tripping up?"

"Yes – how on earth did you know that? You a wizard too?"

I giggled. "I'll tell you how I know – in writing – when you teach me how to read."

"Okay – it's a deal."

He kissed me soundly on the lips and we retired to bed.

*

That night, I dreamed a dream where I skipped through flowered meadows with hundreds of girls racing around and chasing dragons, guarded by elven maidens with sad faces. The girls were so happy. Why were their guards sorrowful? I approached one and asked her.

"We weep for the sorrow of mankind; for the loss of their daughters."

"How were they lost?"

"We took them."

"You? The elves took them? Why? I don't understand."

I was shocked beyond comprehension. The elves? The most benign race ever known? Mysterious, gentle, never seen, only dreamed?

"We take them for safekeeping, allowing just a few to remain so that the race of men may endure."

"But why? What are you keeping them safe from? The dragons are no danger."

"The dragons never were a danger. And now they certainly aren't as you have slain them all."

"But, we – we thought –"

"You thought they were the danger, but you missed the real danger; the 'dragons' in your midst."

"The Sameerdoie?"

"No. They have been forgiven. The evil ones were the traders, the merchants, the traffickers and their allies; the real danger. You miss it still, though the threat has changed. Who spirited away your daughters for the traders?"

"Nobody can 'spirit' away anybody; it's not possible – only the wizards might possibly be able to do that. Jobert? A kindly old wizard who can't even tie his own shoe laces? No. I won't believe it. And anyway, the rich traders are a thing of the past."

"Yes. They have been stopped. The answer is in your dreams."

I woke, upset, wondering. What had the nymph meant? She'd spoken of the ones who spirit away daughters; hinted that the evil ones had been stopped, yet the girls were still being stolen. It couldn't be the wizards, but if not the wizards, then whom? I suddenly felt hot then cold. The elven maiden had told me the answer without me realising it. "We take them" she had said. As simple as that. To safeguard them. From merchants who no longer traded, because there was nothing for them to trade.

The elves. The elves were stealing our children. The elves; beloved creatures of myth.

I smelled wisps of incense on the air. The wizard must be around. I slipped out of bed, wrapped myself in a light robe against the summer morning coolness, and sought the wizard. He was on the battlements, as usual. I told him of my dream. Perhaps there was hope in wizardry. He listened attentively.

"My lady, I thank you. That information is invaluable. Astonishing."

"Jobert, what can we do? How can we fight the elves?"

"Fight the elves? There will be a way, undoubtedly. The problem has always been not knowing who was responsible; not knowing who needed to be stopped. Now we know, we can take action. Leave this to me, my lady. I know the danger now, and know how to fight it. I thank you for this. You don't know how grateful I am." He was close to jumping up and down in his excitement. I'd never seen him like this. "Have you told anyone else?"

"No, just you Jobert", I replied, unthinkingly.

He smiled, raised himself up to his full height, and said in a quiet and matter-of-fact way, "Now, that was a mistake, my lady. I think I might have to arrange a small accident."

"A what?"

"The elven maiden told you more than you realise. The elves really are safeguarding the children. But it wasn't always so."

"No – she spoke of evil traders, and their allies."

"Yes. Their allies." He gave me the familiar kindly smile. "Farewell, my lady."

He raised his hand and started muttering an incantation.

I was transfixed; stupefied. What was he doing? I never found out. Grolland came charging out onto the battlements, sword in hand, towards the wizard.

Jobert turned, laughed, and stepped towards the sword, upraised hand facing Grolland. The centre of his palm started burning with a blue light that increased in intensity rapidly. It formed a shield that the sword glanced off, but Grolland didn't give up. He leapt onto the high wall, presumably thinking he could circumvent the shield that way.

"No Grolland! You'll fall!" I shrieked.

Jobert twisted round to silence me, but in so doing tripped over his shoelaces and stumbled. Grolland wasted no time. He leapt onto the falling wizard and plunged the sword deep between his shoulder blades.

There was a flash of yellow fire, which burnt away Grolland's visor. He stepped back quickly, watching the wizard. Jobert writhed and screamed on the stone flags, consumed, bit by bit by the sulphurous bubbling flame that spread out from the sword wound.

Grolland looked at me. I had never seen his eyes before. They were kindly, dragon's eyes, with triple eyelids.

"I'm sorry my lady. He had to be dispatched. I overheard your conversation. I understood. I knew."

I stood in shock. Grolland was right. And yet... Jobert. My friend. My protector. A traitor? How many more wizards were there? I knew of no others. Perhaps, just perhaps the danger was now gone and the children could return. Would the elves release them now that the last wizard was gone; now that no prospective traders would find an ally for their vile trade? But wizards couldn't be killed. I didn't understand it – yet there was Jobert, turning to a yellowish slime at my feet; clearly dead.

"How, Grolland? How did you kill him? Men cannot kill wizards."

"Men, no. But dragons? Maybe."

He smiled. I met his eyes for the last time, before he produced a new visor from his helmet and covered them again.

He bowed. "My Lady." Then without more ado, he turned and left.

Bolor came running up.

"What the hell is that stench? What...?"

He looked down at the remains of the wizard, and then turned to look at me, speechless for once.

I smiled sweetly, though was unable to still my trembling.

"I've been talking with elves and killing wizards, my love, with the help of a half dragon. Didn't need a mighty barbarian warrior for that, or I'd have called you."

"You did call. You yelped."

"Oh. Yes."

I looked up at him sheepishly, remembering my screech, which had been worthy of my mother upon finding a non-removable stain on some laundry.

Bolor turned his head.

"Listen, love – can you hear them?"

Far away, I could just hear the golden sound of children laughing.

I fixed him with a stern expression. "Just remember. Dragons or no dragons, our daughters must learn to read, write and ride."

He smiled, took my hand, and together we ran down the spiral staircase and out into early morning sun, across the flowered meadow, to greet our daughters.

Gandeel

by Sue Hoffmann

The dragon's laugh rang out across the crowded market square.

"Shut up," hissed Meb, stuffing the pendant back down the neck of her tunic and hastily buttoning her jacket. Muffled chuckles accompanied her as she sauntered towards the jeweller's stall, trying for nonchalance. *"Nothing to do with me,"* she thought, concentrating fiercely and waving her hand as if brushing away a troublesome fly. *"Everything's fine. Nobody heard a thing."*

A muffled guffaw almost spoiled her focus. She thumped a fist into her chest, to be rewarded by a grunt that matched her own slight gasp of pain, then blessed silence. She breathed a sigh of relief and weaved her way onwards.

"Tamas?" she called softly, reaching the stall and seeing a figure crouched over some boxes in the shadows at the rear of the booth.

The young man straightened and came forward. Dark, curling hair framed a heart-shaped face almost feminine but for a hint of strength in jaw and cheekbones, and grey-green eyes met Meb's startled blue gaze.

"Can I help you?" asked the man. "I've new stock in from Urmicka, Lady. A ring, perhaps?" He reached for a glass-covered tray.

"Where's Tamas?"

A slight frown crinkled the man's brow. "Tamas, Lady?"

"Yes, Tamas. Where is he?"

"My apologies, Lady. I don't know anyone of that name."

Panic flared in Meb's stomach. "You must know him. It's his stall. I was told he'd be here…" She floundered to a halt.

"Your pardon, Lady," the man said, a hint of impatience colouring his tone, "but I'm Jayton and I've had this stall for three years now, and you won't find better quality or value in the whole of Lendrin. Now, may I show you some wares, or will you move along and make room for more discerning customers?"

75

Too shaken to bridle at the insult, Meb stumbled away. A herbal-tea vendor had set benches and tables for his customers and Meb sank wearily onto the nearest empty seat. She ordered a mug of feldrax tea with honey and sat cradling it in hands that refused to stop trembling.

The shadows lengthened as curfew approached. Stallholders began to pack away their goods. Meb lifted her rapidly cooling mug and sipped the drink. A hand descended on her shoulder and golden liquid slopped onto the table as she jerked in fright.

"Be still," said a soft voice. "I won't hurt you." The man from the jewellery stall slid his tall frame onto the bench beside her. "You'd better come with me," he said. "Patrols tend to start early around here and they use sentinel hounds."

Meb's heart attempted to beat its way out of her chest. Sentinel hounds. A mild huffing emanated from beneath her tunic and she coughed loudly to cover the sound.

The man's eyes narrowed and he stared thoughtfully at her before stretching casually and pushing himself to his feet. Bending close, his lips brushed her cheek as he whispered, "I can take you to Tamas." Without warning, he took Meb by the waist and swung her from the bench. He snatched up her pack and winked meaningfully at the watching vendor. "I hope your night is as good as mine's going to be," he said, draping an arm around Meb.

Meb stiffened in protest, then changed her mind and allowed herself to be led off towards his booth. Bypassing the front of his shuttered stall, the man took her through a low side door into what was little more than a wooden cubicle with a few cluttered shelves and a blanketed pallet. Suddenly tired of being perpetually frightened, Meb sank to the ground next to the low bed and laid her head on her raised knees. A contented sigh issued forth from the pendant. Meb hastily assayed a coughing fit.

"There's a healer in town if you want to see about that cough," the man said. Meb thought he sounded amused.

He lit an oil lamp then sat down in front of her, holding up the lamp to study her features. Shoving a box aside, he set the lantern safely onto a low shelf. "I'm sorry about earlier," he said. "I couldn't tell you about Tamas. Too many ears and gossiping tongues."

"So you do know him?"

"Oh yes."

Meb felt a shift in the air around her and a gathering of power. Rapidly, the man's figure shifted and blurred - and facing her was an elderly man with reddish-grey hair and beard, deep set brown eyes and the narrow white line of an old scar visible through the stubble on his right cheek. Meb halted her defence spell in mid-flow. The person sitting before her exactly matched the description she had been given of old Tamas. For a moment she forgot to breathe.

"I thought all you Alterants were exiled," she murmured at last.

"And I'd believed all you Karrimar were extinct," he countered.

Meb shrugged her pack higher on her shoulders and quickened her pace to match the long strides of her companion. Questions buzzed in her head like a swarm of angry gapta-flies. She'd wanted answers last evening, but the proximity of the hounds and their handlers had made conversation unwise and, to her great surprise, she'd fallen asleep quickly and slept deeply until first light. She'd woken to find Jayton ready for travel and since she was out of other options, and he *was* Tamas after all, she'd taken the light breakfast he'd offered and had not argued when he'd left his stall closed and had told her to come with him. They'd headed south, away from town, as soon as the release bell sounded.

"So, which are you usually?" Meb asked at last. "Tamas or Jayton?"

Her companion shrugged. "Jayton, mostly. Sometimes Tamas. Now and again Reemer."

Three names? Meb couldn't help staring up at him. Alterants were known to have two personas, but rare indeed was the ability to shift more than that. Rare - and dangerous. Was it not the dual personality that caused the madness for which they'd been exiled? How could he possibly retain his sanity if he had to cope with being *three* people? She'd entrusted herself to the care of a madman! The joyous giggle that came from beneath her clothing could not this time be disguised.

Jayton turned to her and grinned broadly. "Malicious little thing, isn't it?"

Meb felt the colour drain from her face. He'd known all along. Unsure whether to be angry or relieved, she chose the latter. "It's getting harder to control it," she admitted. She unbuttoned her jacket, hooked a thumb through the chain around her neck and drew forth the pendant. "Don't touch it," she warned as Jayton bent to scrutinise the design.

"So that's a *gandeel*? I've heard of them, of course, but seeing one is quite a thrill."

"Glad you think so." She lifted the golden disc by its rim, avoiding the raised motif, and glared at the dragon. Ruby eyes glinted balefully back at her and tiny jaws snapped at her fingers. Meb pulled a face at it and tucked it away again.

Jayton resumed his steady pace and Meb found herself almost trotting to keep up as he led the way off the road and started into the woods to their left.

Suddenly uncomfortable, Meb halted at the edge of the road. "I was told Tamas would help me," she said.

Jayton stopped and turned back. "He will. It's just that I know the way and he doesn't."

A frown creased Meb's brow. She really didn't know enough about Alterants to be able to deal with this. "Well, why don't *you* tell me what I need and then I won't have to trouble either of you any longer?"

Jayton's soft laugh was echoed by the dragon pendant and Meb felt her colour rise.

"No, don't be angry," said Jayton. "I'm not mocking you. Thinking of us as one person is a common misperception. Tamas and I - and Reemer, for that matter - share certain memories and areas of knowledge, else I doubt we'd be able to function, but we each have our own personalities and, in effect, our own lives. There's some communication between us, although that's hard to explain to an outsider. I know them as well as I'd know a close friend or a brother, but I'm not privy to all their secrets."

"So you just … switch? From one to the other?"

"Our lore really is dying out, isn't it?" Jayton mused aloud. "No, we seldom 'just switch'. Most of us can control the change. We alter at will, or at need. Whoever told you to seek out Tamas must have met me *as* Tamas, and apparently it's Tamas who can help you in some fashion. There's a shrine of some sort in the heart of the forest and he wants to go there, so that's where we're going."

"But..."

Jayton's expression hardened. "Enough. I'm losing profit by leaving my stall closed. If you no longer want my aid, say so. I've already given you more than you've a right to demand, Karrimar, and I've received little in return. I don't even know your name."

Meb chewed her lower lip, then tipped her head on one side and smiled coquettishly up at him. "I've shown you my *gandeel*," she said impishly.

Jayton's grey-green eyes widened in surprise, then he threw back his head and roared with laughter. "Come on," he said, wiping away tears of mirth. "If you were directed to Tamas, he probably *can* help you, and we could do with reaching the shrine and being out of the forest again before nightfall."

Meb tapped him on the arm as he was turning away. "I'm Meb," she said.

The deeper they ventured into the woodland, the more apprehensive Meb became. The sounds of the forest were normal enough but she could not shake the feeling of being watched. A slight wavering in the air as they came into a small glade raised the hairs on the back of her neck and she reached forward to grab Jayton's coat.

"What?" he snapped.

"I don't know. I think..."

She had no time to finish voicing her concern. Out of the trees swung dark shapes, long limbs outstretched, wicked claws reaching for her face and eyes. Instinctively she dropped to a crouch, arms over her head. The weight of leathery bodies tumbled her over and she batted wildly at the scratching, clinging creatures.

Something swished perilously close to her left ear. There was a dull squishy sound and the weight on her back and shoulders lessened enough for her to kneel upright.

A tall, broad-shouldered man with flowing red hair danced around her in the glade, his sword and clothing spattered greeny-red with blood from the creatures he fought. Howling with crazy laughter, he ducked from their reach and swung his weapon again and again with deadly accuracy. Meb glanced round frantically for

Jayton, realising as she was about to shout his name that he was, in a way, right there before her. The warrior was dramatically different from the craftsman she had been with just moments ago but the clothing was the same - although now it was tighter across rippling muscles - and even with the ferocious grin there was a distinct similarity of feature. Meb frowned in puzzlement at the sword, though; she could have sworn Jayton carried only a dagger.

He yelled again, a shriek of wild delight, and two more creatures fell dead. Others took their place instantly, and yet more chattered in the branches above, and it was obvious he could not stand against them for much longer. Even as Meb watched in fascinated horror, one of the things almost escaped him on its way towards her. Closing her eyes and striving for inner calm, Meb called upon a spell of fire. Heat gathered in her clenched hands and she loosed the flames in a fiery arc, sending the vicious little beasts screaming away. Bolder than the rest, a few tried to slip under the inferno but a second burst caught them and they fell, shrivelling and smoking. As quickly as they had appeared, the last remaining creatures vanished into the forest and Meb doused the flames before the surrounding vegetation caught ablaze.

Brushing ash from her palms, she turned to see Jayton slumped wearily on a log, wiping sweat from his forehead and grime and gore from his clothing. His face was grey and his mouth set in a thin line of disgust. Meb noticed with some surprise that the sword had gone.

"Are you hurt?" she asked, hastening across the trampled grass.

He shook his head. "A couple of scratches. Nothing more." He rose slowly. "Come on."

Meb grimaced. She wanted to ask about Reemer and the sword, and about Tamas, too, but something in Jayton's expression prevented her. "What were they?" she asked instead.

"Naktari. They're nasty little beasts that attack anything they think might be a source of food. Reemer coped pretty well, though."

"I helped," said Meb, stung that he hadn't even thanked her, let alone mentioned her skill, and faintly sickened by Reemer's apparent enjoyment of the fight. "He... you... he... Oh, shades of night! Whichever you were, I helped."

"Quite right too, since you're the reason we're in this wood. Now, shall we stay here and bicker until they come back with reinforcements, or shall we try for that shrine?"

Biting back a curt retort, Meb gestured theatrically towards the trees ahead. "Do please lead the way. And you can keep quiet, too!"

Jayton frowned, then grinned as he heard the faint chortling from Meb's *gandeel*.

Jayton guided Meb into the heart of the dense forest. Entering a clearing a little larger than the one where they had been attacked, Meb felt her mouth drop open in astonishment at the sight of the shrine. Small though it was, with walls not much higher than Jayton's head, it exuded power. Flowers, trees and animals were painted in vibrant colours all over it, and light glinted from stained-glass windows portraying hills, fields and forests.

"It's beautiful," breathed Meb, heading towards the ornate doorway. "People must know it's here. It's a wonder it hasn't been desecrated."

"Ah, well, there's a reason for that."

A pace away from the entrance, Meb had just registered the fact that it was old Tamas who'd spoken when she was flung away without warning and with a force strong enough to send her flat on her back.

"And that's the reason," said Tamas levelly, strolling over and reaching out a hand to help her up.

"Thanks for the warning," Meb snarled when she had breath to speak again. She dropped her pack to the ground and flexed her shoulders, trying not to stare too hard at the way the soiled clothing now hung loosely on the elderly man's thin frame. "So, how do I get in?"

Tamas scratched at his beard and ambled away to sit in a patch of sunlight, lowering himself gingerly to the lush grass. "That, my dear, is up to you, I'm afraid."
He patted the grass beside him and Meb sighed and went to sit next to him. "Listen, child: I met your father by chance when he was over here selling some of his carvings. I happened to notice he'd a belt buckle of Karrimar design and offered to buy it. Didn't he tell you this?"

"No. But since he still has the buckle, he obviously didn't sell it to you."

"No indeed, despite the exorbitant sum I proposed. He said he had a special interest in such items, so I told him about this place." He jerked his head towards the shrine. "Jayton found it, but I was the one who recognised the designs. From the signs and symbols it would appear the shrine's dedicated to Halathera, the Karrimar goddess of fortune, and it probably contains some valuable artefacts. Your father said he knew someone who'd almost certainly be able to get in, so I suggested we try a joint venture. We arranged to meet at Jayton's market stall - but I must admit I'd expected him to bring that someone with him, not send along a mere child."

"I'm not a child," Meb retorted hotly. "I'm nineteen."

"Yes, well, whatever age you are there'll be no profit for either of us if you can't get in, and that would be a pity. Genuine Karrimaran artefacts can command a tremendous price, young Meb. Especially with the Karrimar being extinct and all that."

Meb ran her fingers through her short curls, wincing as they caught in the tangles. "Jayton knows I'm Karrimar so I bet you know too. If I do find a way in, I'm hardly likely to turn anything over to you to sell, am I?"

The old man shrugged dismissively. "It's obvious the man I met isn't your true father and, yes, of course I know you're Karrimar. I still brought you here, didn't I? Now, are you going to sit squabbling with me or are you going in?"

Meb didn't bother arguing about the wards that had flattened her once already. It was a Karrimar shrine and she was Karrimar: surely it would let her in. She had to know if she was truly the last survivor of her race, and where else could she seek information about her people? Rising quickly, she walked around the little temple, keeping a circumspect distance as she studied the images and inscriptions.

The *gandeel* grew warm against her skin. *Use me to open the shrine,* it seemed to whisper. It would work; she was certain of that. The temptation was strong, stronger then ever before, and she found herself with the *gandeel* in her hand, about to set it against the door and invoke a spell of opening.

Just in time, she realised what she was doing and she thrust the pendant away inside her clothing, heedless of the sting as the dragon nipped her finger in temper. Absently sucking the blood from her fingertip, she made another circuit of the shrine. How could she have thought of squandering the magic like that? An angry sigh and a faintly repulsive wriggle came from the pendant. It had wanted her to waste its power, and its influence was becoming harder to resist. Sooner or later it was likely to win, and that would put and end to all her hopes.

Distracted, she stumbled on the uneven ground. Instinctively she put out a hand to save herself and came into abrupt contact with the door of the shrine. Standing with her spread hand against the sun-warmed wood, Meb tried to work out why she had not this time been flung away by the temple wards. The answer was there before her: visible on the glowing paintwork was a faint smear of blood from her cut finger.

Meb whooped with excitement. "Serves you right," she told the *gandeel* as she pushed open the door and entered the building.

It was dimmer than she had expected, and cooler too, and the austerity inside contrasted starkly with the ornate exterior. Coloured light from the windows painted crazy patterns over plain wooden benches and a simple stone altar. The only icon was a statue of Halathera standing with hands upraised, a young deer at her feet and two tatha-birds on her left shoulder.

Little though she knew of Karrimar traditions and religion, Meb was drawn immediately to the small sculpture. For long moments she stared at the figure, marvelling at the exquisitely carved robe and lifelike features. Even her father's work paled into insignificance next to this.

A yell of pain and surprise jerked her from her contemplation and she spun round to see Tamas sprawled on the grass a few paces outside the shrine's open door. Trying not to laugh, Meb called out, "Mind the wards, Tamas!"

A hearty curse was the response. Smiling, Meb resumed her examination of the little temple. Quite soon, the thrill of discovery faded and disappointment took its place. She had been so sure that there would be something in the shrine, some object or book or scroll, something to tell her what to do next, but apart from the statue there was only an empty flower bowl on one of the narrow window ledges. Forcing back tears of frustration, Meb walked briskly from the shrine. About to close the door, she hesitated, feeling the need to make at least some token offering to Halathera. Leaving the door ajar, and ignoring Tamas sitting nursing a sore arm, she picked a handful of the pretty blue flowers growing prolifically in the glade around the temple, added some greenery and took the little bouquet and her water-bottle back with her into the shrine.

She poured water into the pottery container and then froze in the act of placing the flowers into the bowl. Beneath the water's surface an image was forming, a picture like a map her father had once shown her of Lendrin, with the chain of tiny islands running out into the treacherous Marrakand Sea off the eastern coast. Entranced, Meb watched as the picture shifted, the islands appearing to draw closer until one, the very last in the chain, filled the bowl. Green hills and a fertile valley became visible, with tiny figures moving around what must be a small settlement. Meb leaned forward, eyes wide with astonishment as some of the faces became clearer. Karrimar!

With a gasp, Meb shot upright - and the image faded. When it was apparent the water would show her nothing more, she settled the flowers into the bowl, took a last look at Halathera's calm features and left the temple, this time closing the door firmly behind her.

"Hey!" Tamas was standing as close as he dared to the entrance. "The door, you little fool! What in All Below d'you think you're doing?"

Meb ignored his tirade. She slumped down on the grass and he eased himself onto a convenient tree stump. "I do hope you can get back in there, youngster," he said crossly. "Otherwise I think you and I are about to fall out. A fancy shrine like that wouldn't miss a couple of artefacts now would it?"

"There wasn't anything in there," Meb said. "Only a statue."

"*Only* a statue?"

"It was fixed to the altar, Tamas, and I suspect it had even stronger wards than the shrine itself."

"Well, something's certainly caught your attention."

Meb shrugged. "I think we should go."

She expected argument, but there was a shift in the air around her, a blurring of Tamas's figure, and Jayton was sitting on the tree stump straightening his jacket and smoothing out his trousers. Meb sighed. "I don't think I'm ever going to get used to you doing that."

"Hah! That from a girl who throws fire and then quenches it."

"I suppose you have a point," Meb responded, strangely glad to see Jayton again.

He stood up and bent to retrieve both their packs. Meb snatched hers back, stuffed her water bottle inside and slung it over her shoulder. "I can manage."

"As you wish. Shall we go while there's still plenty of daylight?"

Meb nodded but made no move to follow when Jayton set off. "Jayton," she called, and he turned back. "I saw something in there."

"Oh? Something you want to talk about?"

Meb nodded again. What was it about Jayton that inspired her confidence when she mistrusted Tamas and was positively scared of Reemer?

"I put water in a flower bowl," she began. Jayton waited patiently and she found the words came easily. "It turned into sort of a scrying bowl and it showed me the Marrakand Islands. They're supposed to be uninhabited, aren't they?"

"Uninhabited and uninhabitable," Jayton confirmed.

"That's what I thought. But there are people on the most easterly one. And, Jayton - they're Karrimar."

A moment's silence passed before Jayton said gently, "It must be a bit overwhelming for you, finding a Karrimar shrine like this. You probably *imagined* seeing your people, or maybe if you truly saw a vision it was from the past. Your people are gone, Meb."

Meb shook her head in denial, her dark curls bouncing. "No, Jayton. It was real and it was now."

Jayton scratched at an insect bite on his neck. "The look on your face suggests you're planning something stupid, Meb."

"It's not stupid to want to find your own people," Meb retorted.

"Perhaps not - *if* they're really there. But tell me this: how do you propose to make your way undetected through Lendrin and out to the island to find out?"

Meb's engaging smile turned her features from merely pretty to stunning. "You'll help me, won't you, Jayton?"

At first, Jayton didn't reply. He tugged thoughtfully at his lower lip. "I know some fishermen who might take us out there," he said at last, "but we'd have to get to the harbour in Ulvern."

"The capital city?"

Jayton nodded. "Trouble is, the city gates are warded against Alterants."

"I could get us in," Meb declared.

"Well then, if you're sure you can do it…"

"You'll really help?"

He swore out loud, then forced a laugh. "Yes," he said. "And may your goddess Halathera protect her wayward child and the idiot who accompanies her!"

*

"So your mother left you the *gandeel*?"

"Yes." Meb settled back against the padded seat of the wagon and revelled in the beauty of the open countryside. It seemed they'd been sneaking through towns and villages for months rather than just six days, and having clear sky above and no habitation in sight sent her spirits soaring. She had even begun to volunteer information to Jayton, something she'd have considered unthinkable a week ago. Jayton clucked softly to the pony and the sturdy little beast quickened her pace. "Go on," he prompted when Meb lapsed into silence.

"Well, my mother was overseas in Chapancia when the plague struck and, as far as I know, she was the only Karrimar out of the country at the time."

"And that's why she didn't fall ill like the rest?"

"It must have been, mustn't it? While she was in Chapancia she discovered she was pregnant and when the news reached her about the Karrimar plague she stayed abroad until I was born."

"But she didn't remain with you?"

"No. She believed she could help our people, and she wanted to find out what had happened to my father, so she left me with Ellini and Gopa and sailed back to Lendrin."

"And you found this out when?"

"Three years ago. My mother had spelled me to keep me safe but when I turned sixteen my powers started to manifest themselves. My parents - I mean Ellini and Gopa - told me the truth then, and they've helped me as much as they can. On Gopa's last trip here he met Tamas and learned about the shrine, and that's why I came. Apparently there were never very many Karrimar, but I have to know if I'm really the last one."

"You're taking a chance on the plague though, aren't you?"

Meb shrugged. "I doubt it's still active after all these years, especially since there are no Karrimar to pass it on. If I'm wrong, then I'll be joining my people anyway, won't I? Either way, I win."

"That's one way to look at it," agreed Jayton with a grimace. "And the *gandeel*?"

"I don't actually know all that much about it," Meb admitted. "Apparently *gandeels* are very rare and they're the most powerful artefacts the Karrimar ever made. They're almost sentient. This one woke when my powers began to develop so it's linked to me and will work for me, if I can control it. It seems to have acquired a mind of its own along the way. Ellini and Gopa could only give me the few instructions my real mother had left."

"And they were?"

"Keep it hidden. Make it obey. Use it only once."

"That's somewhat cryptic. Still, I see now why you didn't use it against those flying things in the forest or to get into the shrine. Anyway, your own spells seem to have done the job in keeping us unnoticed. Being self-taught and having to learn about your magic by trial and error must have been hard, though. You've done well, Meb."

Meb twisted round and fussed with the provisions in the back of the cart, hiding the ridiculous flush of pride that he'd actually praised her. When her skin cooled and she turned back to find him grinning at her she reddened again, this time with anger.

"Why are you here?" she asked.

Jayton's grin faded and he frowned. "What?"

"Why are you here?" Meb repeated.

"I'm helping you. Exactly why is as much a mystery to me as it is to you."

Meb thought he sounded strangely defensive. "I didn't mean that. Alterants are exiles. It's probably more dangerous for you to be here than it is for me."

"About the same, I reckon," Jayton said. He tugged his hat lower to shade his eyes. "Tamas is the one for tales. Ask him next time you see him."

Meb chose not to pursue the matter. Even in Chapancia everyone knew the story of how the Alterants had once been the elite guard of Lendrin's royal family, until the guard captain had fallen prey to the madness and killed King Halkin and his daughter. Heartbroken, and fearful for her young son, Queen Annella had banished every Alterant from Lendrin.

In some ways the events paralleled the fall of the Karrimar, for they too had been in service to the royal house of Lendrin until the plague had struck them down not long after the departure of the Alterants. And in the same manner as Annella had replaced the whole guard unit with protectors brought in from her own country, so had she employed some of her father's mages as substitutes for the once powerful Karrimar sorcerers. She'd brought in the curfew, too, and the patrols with their sentinel hounds. Meb had once overheard Gopa voice the opinion that the old king should never have married again after the death of his first wife, but as long as the young king and his mother had no designs upon Chapancia he supposed it was no concern of his.

Could it be, Meb wondered, that Queen Annella had not been as devastated by the loss of her husband as was widely believed, but that she had actually been paving the way for her son to inherit the throne? If so, then perhaps the wrong person had been blamed for the attack upon King Halkin - and that might just begin to explain why Alterant Jayton was risking his life by being in Lendrin.

The wagon jounced over a rut and Meb grabbed the side bar to avoid being flung out. She gasped and swore as she bounced back onto her seat, but the expletive had less to do with the jolt than with the sudden thought that maybe the Karrimar plague had not been a natural disaster. If the queen could stoop to murdering her own husband and stepdaughter, she would hardly be averse to eliminating the very people who'd undoubtedly oppose the use of foreign guards and mages. And what would Annella do if she discovered an Alterant and a Karrimar about to enter Lendrin's capital city? Against Meb's chest, the *gandeel* grew warm. Was it warning her of coming danger or confirming her suspicions about the Karrimar plague? Or was it merely reminding her of its presence and growing strength? Meb sighed and rubbed gently at the irritation on her skin.

Jayton timed it well. The evening was drawing on as they approached the city gates and the traffic on the roadway increased considerably over the last mile or so as people hurried to enter before curfew and lockout. Meb's *we're innocent traders returning to our shop* incantation saw them safely past the warded gates and the sentries, although she almost lost her concentration when one of the sentinel hounds bayed as they trundled away down the cobbled street towards the harbour.

Jayton had been strangely quiet for the past hour or so and he remained silent as he guided the pony into the stable yard of a shabby waterfront inn. A horrid suspicion rose within Meb. "You're using me," she said suddenly.

"What?"

"You don't really intend to help me. You just wanted a way into the city, and I provided that."

Jayton stared at her without answering.

"You said you'd help me find a boat. You're not going to, are you?"

He shook his head. "I'm sorry, Meb." Looping the reins around the cart rail, he jumped lightly down and held out a hand for her. Disdaining his offer, she scrambled down herself.

"Look," he said, "there's an inn called *Gannybird's Nest* just a little further along the waterfront. You should be safe there while you decide what to do. I'd ask you to stay here but I've some business to attend to and one or two of the people I'm meeting might ask awkward questions if they see you. You'll need to hurry though. It's not far off curfew."

She didn't enquire about what he was planning, nor did she offer any farewell. The betrayal stung too deeply for words. She took her pack from the cart and headed briskly out of the stable yard.

She had gone but a short way when the stamp of booted feet and the baying of hounds halted her and brought her out in a cold sweat. Curfew hadn't sounded yet; why was a patrol heading this way? She ducked into a nearby doorway and pressed herself against the wood. *"I'm not here,"* she whispered, concentrating fiercely. *"Don't see me. Don't smell me."* The spell would work on the guards, but what about the hounds?

Relief weakened her knees as the patrol passed by and totally ignored her. Stepping from the doorway, she saw the sentries halt outside the inn she'd just left. Two guards took one of the hounds around to the stable yard while the other four headed for the front door. A tall man in green robes preceded this latter group and from the aura surrounding him Meb guessed he must be one of the king's mages. She felt sick. Her disguise was good and her spells strong but Jayton, with his Alterant magic, had detected her Karrimar features. How much easier would it be for a powerful mage to sense her presence? He hadn't stopped, though, had he? And presumably he had no reason to suspect a Karrimar was close by. They must be after Jayton, and the mage had failed to notice her because he was intent on some magic of his own.

Confirmation came swiftly. Shouts and crashes, the bloodcurdling howl of the hounds, and a yell of pain came from the inn, and Meb cowered back into her doorway as Jayton was dragged out into the street. Why didn't he "change"? Surely Reemer could break those ropes easily. Then she saw the mage, hands raised, lips moving. She hadn't known there was a spell that could prevent an Alterant from "changing", but then there was a great deal she didn't know about her own magic let alone other powers.

Indecision tore at Meb's heart. She wanted to follow as Jayton was led away but she had to find a boat to take her out to that island. Surely her own people were more important than a renegade Alterant who'd duped her with a false promise of help? She took two steps in the direction of the waterfront and halted. Jayton had been betrayed too, hadn't he? Someone he was counting on meeting must have informed the authorities, and Jayton faced certain death.

Keeping back as far as she could without losing sight of them, Meb trailed the patrol. Once, rounding a corner, she came too close and one of the hounds turned and snarled and the guard holding the beast's leash glanced round. Meb froze. The curfew bell sounded and the guard tugged the animal onwards, leaving Meb sweating with terror.

With the streets empty there was a much greater chance of being spotted, but the patrol seemed focussed on their prisoner and the mage was still muttering his spells as he hastened along. Meb kept going.

No opportunity presented itself to free Jayton quickly, and all too soon the tall railings and elaborate gates of what could only be the royal palace came into view at the top of a tree-lined avenue. Lights ringed the metal fencing and armed sentries stood on duty. Peering round one of the trees, Meb saw Jayton stumble and fall. Someone hauled him upright and shoved him on.

Meb clutched the rough bark and fought back tears. She stood no chance of getting through those gates. Jayton was lost to her. She was surprised at how much that hurt.

A commotion halted her just as she was about to head back to the harbour. Bugles blared out a fanfare, and a lighted procession came out through the opened gates and halted by the patrol. From a gilded carriage stepped a richly-dressed figure. Lamplight glinted on the golden circlet that bound the man's blond hair as he assisted down an older woman. The man's words carried clearly to where Meb hugged the tree trunk.

"So this is what an Alterant looks like," he sneered. "I'd expected something more." He turned to the patrol leader and the mage. "I'm due at the mayor's ball. Keep him safe for me until tomorrow." He extended his arm to the woman. "Come, Mother."

Meb barely had time to register the fact that she was seeing Lendrin's king and his mother when an outpouring of power blurred the air as Jayton disappeared and Reemer took his place. The mage was the first to die, his magic no match for the formidable Alterant, and two of the guards went down within seconds. Ignoring the straining hounds, the guards and his own wounds, Reemer shrieked with berserk laughter as he lunged for Queen Annella. His intention was clear, and Meb knew in that instant that this had been Jayton's plan all along.

91

He almost succeeded. His sword was at Annella's throat when three guards leapt onto his back and brought him crashing down. Weapons upraised, two more guards raced forward.

"Don't kill him, you fools!" the king thundered. "Take him alive! I want him alive!"

It would be worse for him than dying here; Meb knew that with absolute certainly. That Jayton had made use of her talents mattered not at all right at this moment. Without him and Tamas and Reemer she would never have learned that some Karrimar still lived. And without Jayton, something would be forever missing from her life. The *gandeel* throbbed and thudded against Meb's skin, begging for its magic to be released and this time she willingly gave in. Yanking the pendant out so hard that the chain scored her neck, she opened herself to its power.

The dragon roared and the world went mad. Black clouds billowed directly overhead and forked lightning lanced down again and again. Swirling winds swept up dust, leaves and branches and huge hailstones pelted down like an avalanche of rocks. The two hounds fled yelping in terror as their handlers fell dead, and the panicked horses bolted back into the palace grounds, the sumptuous carriage jouncing behind them. Screams of pain and terror rent the air as the unnatural storm continued its deadly work. Meb fought for mastery of the *gandeel* but it was too strong for her unpractised art. Vainly, she tried to direct the lightning's flow to avoid Reemer but the *gandeel* would not relinquish its rule and she could not prevent the mass slaughter. Only when she saw the king and his mother struck down did she drop the pendant in shock.

The storm abated as swiftly as it had begun. Too late Meb realised that she had held the magic in place by keeping her hands on the dragon disc. There had been a way to control it after all, if only she had been properly taught. The dragon sniggered, sighed, and was silent.

Fighting nausea and trembling limbs, Meb staggered to where she had last seen Reemer. She hadn't saved him after all, just bought him a swifter death. An arm in a familiar red sleeve poked out from beneath a pile of bodies and tears streamed unheeded down Meb's cheeks as she struggled to roll the dead guards off Reemer's body. The arm twitched and sudden desperation lent her strength.

Freed from the press of bodies, Reemer groaned and rolled slowly into a sitting position. Blood coated him like a second skin. He saw Meb then, and a wide grin split his face, white teeth gleaming incongruously against the gore spattering his cheeks. He seemed about to speak, but his whole frame shook, blurred and shifted until it was Tamas sitting there.

"We have to go," the old man said. "There'll be more guards here soon, and the city watch, too. Don't just stand there, child. Help me up."

She could never have managed Reemer - or Jayton, for that matter - but Tamas seemed to have a wiry strength of his own and she was able to get him to his feet and support him away from the carnage around the palace gates. Somehow, they made it to the harbour without discovery and Meb half-dragged, half-carried the elderly man into a derelict warehouse. She covered him with old sacking and sprawled, panting, next to him. Whispering a *we're not here* spell, she made ready to keep watch - and fell asleep through sheer exhaustion.

The next three days were a living nightmare for Meb. With the city in chaos, she would have preferred to stay hidden but at times she was forced to leave the warehouse to find food and water and whatever basic medicines she could buy without arousing suspicion. Maintaining her magical protection over the warehouse and herself taxed her powers to their very limit. What scared her most was the way the wounded Alterant shifted from one form to another, sometimes lucid but more often than not delirious with fever. Worst of all, though, the instructions her birth-mother had left concerning the *gandeel* kept playing over and over in her head: "Use it only once."

Under her clothing, the dragon disc lay cool and inert, its power spent, and Meb had lost her only way of reaching her people. They were there on the island, she was convinced of it. Those few who had survived the plague would have needed somewhere remote where they could hide until their numbers grew and their magic was strong enough for them to return. With the *gandeel*, she could have crossed the treacherous sea and joined them. She felt empty, drained, a dried husk. Only the need to tend Jayton kept her from utter despair.

She woke on the fourth morning to find Tamas, clear eyed and alert, sitting chewing a rather stale piece of bread.

"Is this the best you could find?" he grumbled, and Meb's temper flared before she realised he was teasing. "Sit down, child," he said. "You look worse than I feel."

"I thought I'd lost you," Meb said, sliding down beside him.

"Not yet," he said. "Not yet."

"Tamas...?"

The laughter lines around his eyes crinkled as he smiled. "What happens if one of us dies?"

Meb nodded.

"Well, we all die, of course."

"But you're..."

"Old?" he finished for her.

She nodded again.

"One persona sometimes ages more quickly in an Alterant," he explained. "Once a certain age is reached, though, the process slows until the other catches up - or *others*, in my case."

"So..."

"So you won't lose Jayton just because I'm older."

Meb coloured.

"Speaking of whom..." said Tamas. The air around him shimmered and Jayton took his place.

Rage and relief made Meb's tone sharp. "You planned this all along," she accused. "Revenge. You just wanted revenge."

Jayton sighed wearily. "Not just revenge, Meb. With Annella dead, there'd be a chance for us, for my people. We're no danger to Lendrin. Just the opposite. In time, we could send ambassadors to the king. Convince him of our value. We could come home."

Meb's laugh was harsh. "Dreamer!" she scoffed. "What made you think the king would listen after an Alterant had killed his mother?"

"It doesn't matter," Jayton said. "Nothing matters now. I failed, didn't I?"

"That depends on how you define failure. Annella's dead, Jayton. So's her son."

She told him then about following him to the palace, about Reemer's fight and about the *gandeel*. He listened in shocked silence.

"I'll help you get out of the city," she said. "After that..." she trailed off. After that, what? She was more alone than Jayton. He had Tamas and Reemer, and other Alterants in other countries. She had no one.

"I'm sorry," Jayton said gently. "I'm sorry I dragged you into this, and I'm sorry about the *gandeel*. You can't use it again, can you?"

Meb shook her head. "I'm going to come back, though," she said with sudden determination. "I'm not giving up."

"Good for you. I'll help if I can. Really, Meb. Once things have settled down here, we'll both come back, and we'll find a way to reach that island of yours."

Meb leaned against the wooden wall. "It might have succeeded," she murmured. "Your plan, I mean. If the Karrimar were here, they'd have worked with the Alterants to restore the throne to a rightful ruler. The old king had a niece, didn't he? I wonder where she is? Jayton, d'you think..." But Jayton had fallen asleep.

The following morning, Jayton insisted he was well enough to travel and Meb packed up their meagre belongings ready for the journey. They left at dawn, aiming to be at the city gates as soon as they opened.

No patrols roamed the harbour this day, and fisher folk went about their early morning business as if nothing momentous had happened. Meb and Jayton paused at the harbour wall to watch as two small ships sailed in on the morning tide. Only as the vessels drew close did Meb sense the haze of power surrounding them. Gripping Jayton's arm so tightly that he yelped, she raised her free hand to shade her eyes against the glare of sun on water. The first ship docked, a lithe figure leaping ashore to tie a mooring rope around a bollard. He turned to survey the harbour and Meb saw clearly his Karrimar features.

Jayton's mouth dropped open. "Karrimar?" he whispered.

Joy lit Meb's face. "Oh, yes," she breathed.

"But how...? Why...?"

95

"The *gandeel*," said Meb. "They sensed its power. They know what's happened, and they've come home."

With one hand clutching the spent *gandeel* and the other tightly clasped in Jayton's warm fingers, she went to meet her people.

Little Teeth

by Jenny Black

The air outside The Seventh Son Lounge was bejewelled with drizzle, and inside it was draped in smoke. It was open mic night, and at the small corner stage a gremlin sat on a bar stool and played Spanish guitar. The sum of all non-human life was there, with a smattering of human customers thrown in for good measure - hoary wisemen and dreamy priestesses, courtly seers and shabby shamen. A young gentleman was seated up by the bar, wearing an off-white hybrid between a ceremonial robe and a lab coat. His name was Johan, and Johan was an alchemist. If it was not given away by his speech, this fact could usually be gleaned from the sulphur stained smock, studded with burns, that he habitually wore over his jeans (apparently there had once been some attempt at gold brocade, which had long since caught fire), and the fact that every attempt by his eyebrows to grow back was thwarted by constant singeing.

Johan perched on the edge of a tall stool, his tousled head bent over a garish blue drink as he scribbled something, most likely esoteric and at least slightly arcane, on a scrap of paper. Next to him sat a man of startling grey-green pallor, mottled with tiny scales which reflected the colours around him whenever he moved his shimmering head. His name was Douglas, and he often drank with Johan, although technically it was more osmosis than actual drinking; his webbed fingers soaked in a Martini as he peered over at his friend. Johan covered the paper quickly.

"It's not finished yet man, don't look!"

"Jo, we're in a bar, relax for two seconds." Douglas *did* have an incredibly relaxing voice, the vocal equivalent of running water. That was one of the reasons the highly-strung Johan liked him, although one found oneself vaguely needing the toilet after lengthy conversations with the nymph. Douglas generally didn't have a clue what Johan was saying, but he liked to listen.

"It's alright for you, you're all Albedo, you're way ahead of me. Perhaps I should stop drinking, it can't be very purifying."

Polishing a glass absently, Rex the hairy bartender laughed good naturedly to himself at overhearing this. Johan looked at him ruefully, downed his drink and called for another.

He jumped nearly out of his seat as Douglas laid a cool hand on his shoulder. "Leave it in the lab, Jo. I swear you'll die of stress, if you don't blow yourself up first." Limpid eyes regarded Jo's drawn face, "You know, you're so jumpy people will think you're up to something."

The scientist slumped on his seat and leant heavily on the bar. "Doug, what I wouldn't... I've told you, I just attract trouble. Something about me just offends the fates."

"That is such bollocks. If the fates met you they'd like you very much, you're just paranoid."

"No I'm serious. It's as if the universe -" The lament was cut short as, during a flourish of his arm intended to indicate the general universe, Johan's hand collided with something. He heard a shattering of glass and was suddenly aware of something ominous and muscle-bound standing behind him. He turned round slowly, a hot dread creeping up the back of his neck, and found himself facing what appeared to be lots of mouthless little teeth. The sight of them stirred something in him, a primal fear he had not felt since childhood; the solid fear that children feel alone at night in the dark, when the shadows form all the monstrous shapes of young imaginings.

When Johan was small, he had never been afraid of the dark like other children were. His insatiable curiosity meant that, if something went bump in the night, he would go and find out what it was. If he was told a story to frighten him, he would deliberately push his luck to see if that story was true. His favourite hobby was dismantling things to see how they worked - VCRs, hairdryers, dead animals - whatever he got his hands on. Even at that early age things blew up or electrocuted him quite often, but the word 'deterrent' was not yet in his vocabulary.

No, Johan was not afraid of the phantoms in his imagination. He was afraid of monsters. He knew they were real, and he had seen them. Though now he lived among them, that first encounter was entrenched in his subconscious, and though he had forgotten the details, he still remembered what was important.

He was pulled from his trance by Douglas' voice beside him. "We're so sorry," he was saying hurriedly, "are you alright?"

Johan's senses began to kick in and he found himself adding, "Yes, I'm really sorry, can I buy you another drink?" His mouth moved automatically as his eyes panned up and down the figure that stood before him and he began to make sense of what he saw. He was confronted by a lean and muscular man nearly seven feet tall, wearing heavy boots, heavy trousers and some form of leather armour lashed over the top of the whole ensemble. One hand was still holding an invisible glass, and studded gauntlets strapped over his forearms extended down over his knuckles. A pair of slightly crushed and ragged wings, like those of a huge, bedraggled moth, were visible extending behind and above the figure, framing a large head set on broad shoulders. The face also had weight to it, with low brows and a mean mouth, and ears curling and tapering to high points. Around his neck he wore several heavy necklaces, like grim trophies, which hung down his chest, as well as several more tied to a thick belt at his waist; long strings of threaded human teeth.

Apparently, Douglas' usually soothing manners had no effect on the man, who seemed barely to notice him and instead directed a constant weighty glower at Johan, to whom everything about the creature was suddenly sickeningly familiar.

"You," began the towering fae figure, "have spilled my pint."

"Yes, I'm very sorry!" Johan found his eyes gravitating back to the strings of teeth, despite his best efforts. They were small teeth, white and blunt. The fae caught the direction of his gaze and leaned closer.

"These," he lifted one of the strings so it dangled hypnotically in front of Johan's face, "are all the teeth of the people who's teeth I have punched out."

Johan gaped haplessly. He'd been threatened plenty of times before, but there was something important about the teeth, something on the edge of memory...

In a far corner of his mind, a cold dread was seeping through. It was a feeling Johan remembered from when he was a small boy. He remembered watching a shadow in the darkness of his room so intently that he almost didn't notice when it started to move. The black bulk rose up and took the shape of a huge figure with terrible ragged wings, silhouetted against the faint blue light from he window. He could see the glint of metal, and something else. He had pulled the covers up so only his eyes peeped over the duvet, and watched with horror as the thing began to approach. It moved quietly, almost silently, but for a slight clacking sound, like beads bumping together.

A few of the other patrons had turned to watch, but no one was paying them any special attention. Johan and Douglas looked at one another and then back at the hostile individual squared up before them. Rex leaned purposefully on the counter, looking at the newcomer with canny eyes. He placed another drink in front of the man, bared his wicked teeth and growled deep in his throat. The drink was accepted and the fae began to back off. He shook his finger at Johan and looked for a moment as if he was trying to frame some sort of threat, but eventually settled on just poking the beleaguered young man hard in the chest before stalking off across the room.

Panic subsiding, the two friends turned back to face the bartender. Johan opened his mouth to say thank you but was waved off with a cheery, "Don't mention it!"

Douglas sought for something positive to say, but nothing presented itself at that moment so he stuck his fingers back in his drink and smiled awkwardly.

"Am I doomed?" Johan wondered aloud.

"Hey, don't worry about it. He talks loud enough but he probably wasn't going to follow through, just wanted to look tough. He'll forget about us before the end of the night."

Johan smiled feebly. It was very sweet of Douglas to pretend they were in it together, but he couldn't help but feel seriously exposed.

"Can we just get out of here?" he said to his friend.

"No way. You can't let him bully you out of here, it's not as though it's *his* bar, is it? If people like us kept letting people like him get away with it, where would we be?"

Johan's slightly latent sense of honour told him Doug was right, but he also had a less latent sense of not wanting to see his molars converted into jewellery.

"Alright, but please let's not sit at the bar anymore. I feel really conspicuous up here."

Douglas nodded and the two of them gathered their drinks and their coats and wandered off into the bar proper.

Five minutes later they had managed to acquire two low and very squashy armchairs set up around a tall hookah in one corner of the room. There were three other chairs all occupied by pixies, but they were lying back staring at the ceiling with rapt concentration and intermittent giggling.

Douglas blew smoke out of his nose and then puffed more out of the gills on his neck, wreathing his head in curling tendrils. Johan watched him idly and felt like he was looking at his friend underwater. He recovered his train of thought and, though the smoke had dulled him physically, he found that if he concentrated he could access parts of his mind usually elusive when his head was clear.

"That guy is watching me I know it." he muttered with some effort.

"Ignore him," Douglas sighed in return, "Don't think about it or you'll freak out."

"I've seen him before I'm sure of it. I've seen those little teeth..." He sat up suddenly, and then regretted it as the head rush hit him. But through the haze of memory, something was coming back, a thought that had been driving him without him knowing it. He remembered how he had seen his first monster.

As he was drifting off to sleep, he heard a thump from the darkness of his room. His eyes darted from corner to corner but he could make nothing out in the gloom. His eyes fell upon the shadow of a chair draped with clothes, and he squinted to see if the impression of a hulking shape against the wall was just cast by an old jumper. Then the demon had stepped out of hiding and begun to edge towards him.

The creature had got closer and closer; Johan could just see the familiar, but not quite placeable, shapes of the beads it wore as they clicked on their long strings. The creature reached out a hand towards the pillow, it came towards Johan in slow motion, though didn't seem to be reaching for *him*. As the monster leaned over, the necklaces dangled forwards and Johan realised what they were made from. He let out a shrill scream and screwed up his eyes, and the creature started and withdrew hastily. Johan heard footsteps from the landing outside his room and the door began to open. He looked around quickly but the nightmare was gone, just as if it had never been, and his mother came into the room, flooding it with light and safety.

But Johan has been petrified, and nothing could convince him that his monster wasn't real. From then on he read voraciously, books of magic and folklore, determined to learn a secret that would keep him safe from monsters forever. From there he had become a scholar of alchemy, seeking a way to control his fear and its cause.

He gripped Douglas' hand suddenly, and sat bolt upright in wide-eyed panic.

"Ow! What are you playing at? I need those fingers!" Douglas exclaimed with indignance. Johan didn't let go though, and pulled his friend round to face him.

"He *is* after me!"

"Oh not this again."

"No he is, he's always been after me!"

"Jo, you are freaking right out. Let me get you a glass of water."

"A pox on your water! This is serious! When I was about eight years old, that guy, it *had* to have been him, came to get me. I think he was going to eat me or something, but I raised the alarm just in time. I couldn't remember it until just now, it was too much for a child to think about."

"You are serious, aren't you?"

"Deadly serious. We have to get out of here. Maybe leave the country, I'm not sure yet." Johan pulled Douglas towards the door, but when he looked behind him he saw the creature from his nightmares glance over at him. "Shit. No, we have to stay. We're safer where there's people, if we go out there he'll follow us and kill me in some dark ally. Rex won't let him get me as long as we're in here."

Douglas rolled his eyes as he was dragged back towards the bar, where he slumped into a seat.

"Alright, calm down and everything will be alright." He leaned over the counter and called to the barmaid who was serving with Rex that night. Momentarily she placed two large glasses of scotch in front of them and smiled as she took money from Douglas. Johan raised his glass with trembling hands and gulped down the liquor.

"Sorry love, could we get two more?" Doug asked the girl when she brought him his change. Upon receipt of the drinks he gathered them up and led Johan over to a discreet table to talk him round.

Last orders had long since been called and the lounge was emptying, while still they sat at their table. Douglas made several attempts to leave, complaining that they couldn't stay there all night, but Johan was quite adamant they could, and wouldn't move or let the winged aggressor out of sight.

Rex ambled over and looked at them pointedly, hands on his hips above his novelty *pac-man* belt. "Time, gentlemen."

Johan peered round him at the figure in the corner. "Rex man, we can't leave. Look at him, he's going to ambush me!"

"What?"

"That guy, that guy over there, he wants my teeth, look at him."

"Him? Martin?" Rex looked over his shoulder and smiled. "He's not going to hurt you, you silly clot."

"What do you mean? You saw him!"

Rex pulled a chair over and sat down, leaning forward conspiratorially. "The thing about Martin is, he's a tooth fairy. He got those teeth from children who left them under their pillows for him, he leaves coins, and every six months he takes them all in to head office and exchanges them for his pay slip, and goes back and builds up another few necklaces." Johan and Douglas looked at each other, "He really wouldn't hurt a fly, they vet you for things like that before

103

you can get the job. He's pretty embarrassed about it though, hence the whole hardman act. He hates the term tooth fairy, calls himself a 'dental recycling operative'. Ludicrous, but it's best just to play along really, he can get so depressed."

"Really? He's harmless?"

"Sure. He's an alright fellow really, a bit paranoid but he's alright."

Johan flushed with embarrassment and a wide smile spread across Douglas' features.

"Oh. Right then."

"Yeah. So pack up and go home, I can't leave until you do."

"… Thanks Rex."

They got to their feet and Douglas laughed, taking Johan's arm in his as they wandered towards the door.

The bartender grinned to himself as he wiped the table and upturned the chairs on top of it, then betook himself off to see to the other stragglers.

When Johan farewelled his friend and returned to his small apartment, he took down a tiny wooden box from high on a closet shelf. He looked inside and smiled at the heap of little milk teeth that lay indifferently in the bottom; he hadn't quite been able to remember why he had kept them for so long, but it has seemed important that he guard them. He took the lid off the box and left it open on his bedside table, before he turned off the light and went to sleep. In the morning it was empty, save for a shiny pile of 20p coins.

Comic by Jenna Whyte

The Doom of Mournshire

by Benjamin Sperduto

It was always a good idea to bring a witch along on dangerous journeys. The morning's ambush had cost Narim six of the fifteen mercenaries he had hired in Nemdris but more would have been lost without Ilesha's aid. Her collection of healing herbs, potions, and pastes that looked unhealthy and smelled even fouler had quickly won their trust and pushed aside their fears of her witchcraft. It came as little surprise to Narim, for most of them had also come to trust him and with far less reason.

Narim watched Ilesha closely and found it difficult to be unaffected by her presence. She was quite beautiful, though the features of her lean face were not unlike those of a cunning bird of prey that studied its victim intently before striking the killing blow. Her manner was cold, calculating, and grim; all the qualities Narim admired in a woman.

"It seems the witch has finished her work."

Narim turned to face an auburn haired woman who was quite different from Ilesha. Her tall, muscular frame towered over him and she regarded him with icy blue eyes set menacingly within her wolfish face. Her name was Serafima, a fearsome warrior from the barbaric land of Rostogov.

"And?"

"Two of them are still bloody and cleaved; no use to us in battle. I trust that the loss of eight swords will not doom this venture of yours?"

Narim had grown tired of her impertinence. Were it not for the fact that her blade alone was worth almost as much as his other mercenaries combined he might have already slit her throat in the night.

"Are the others ready to move on?" Narim asked.

"They're well enough to travel."

Narim noticed that Serafima had not permitted Ilesha to touch the minor cut she had sustained in the fight with the bandits.

"Ilesha should tend to that."

Serafima grunted. Narim surmised that the superstitious barbarian would rather bleed to death than allow a witch to touch her.

"Lucien has gone ahead to scout the valley," Serafima said.

"The fool wastes his time. He knows not what he seeks," Narim said.

Ilesha walked over to join them. Although she was more than a head shorter than Serafima, she was still tall enough to look down at Narim. As she came to his side, he noticed she was careful to avoid getting too close to Serafima.

"Gather your things," he said, "we're moving on. Mournshire awaits us."

Lucien emerged from the thick underbrush as Narim, Ilesha, and Serafima approached the valley that ran through the heart of the forest like an ugly gash that refused to heal. The rabble of mercenaries followed close behind them.

"I can't find a way down, Narim," Lucien said.

Lucien pulled a patch of briars aside, giving the others a clear view of the valley. Its walls were steep, plunging almost straight down before disappearing beneath a thick blanket of mist.

"Not fog," Ilesha said, "steam."

The witch had heretofore spoken little and Lucien seemed startled by the sound of her silken voice.

"It is said that whatever sorcery destroyed this place affected the temperature of the valley," she said. "The hot air of the valley turns to steam when it rises to the much colder surface."

"A pity that bit of knowledge doesn't help us reach the bottom," Serafima said.

Narim reached into his cloak to pull out a green jewel encircled by three gold bands. It emitted faint waves of heat when exposed to the frigid air. Serafima watched him closely.

"What is that?" she asked.

"A trinket I happened to acquire in the course of my trade, nothing more," he said.

Narim tossed the jewel into the bramble thickets that surrounded the ridge of the valley. It fell through them, but in doing so took hold of the dense, thorny vines and pulled them along as it descended. The underbrush fell in upon itself as branches and roots from all around the valley's edge formed a walkway reaching down into the steamy depths of the valley.

He met Serafima's suspicious glare.

"It would be better if you did not know."

Lucien led the way down the sloping walkway of intertwined branches and roots, his bow at the ready. Serafima followed close behind with her big broadsword. Next in the procession were three of the hired swords, Narim, and Ilesha. The rest of the mercenaries followed behind them.

The temperature rose steadily as they drew closer to the thick mist rising from the unseen valley floor. They were beginning to sweat by the time Lucien reached the upper portions of the steam cloud. He hesitated at first, then took a few steps forward and disappeared into the mist. Serafima scowled and grunted before following him.

The mercenaries, however, seemed reluctant to approach the mist. One of the men even poked at it with his drawn sword as if he expected it to twitch.

"Get moving, you sods!" Narim said, ushering them forward.

As they marched deeper into the valley, the thick mist cleared slightly. Narim could discern the lumbering shape of the hired swords a few feet in front of him, then Serafima and Lucien. He noticed that Lucien was no longer descending and had stepped off to the side of the path to wait for the others to join him.

The air was thick with humidity and the heat almost unbearable. They wasted little time stripping away their heavy winter garments, which were already soaked with sweat. The ground was soft and muddy.

"Like a bloody swamp down here," someone said.

"Be silent!" Narim said. "You needn't announce our presence to whatever evil still lingers within these mists."

Narim turned to see Lucien examining the ground a few yards ahead of them.

"What is it? What has he found?" he asked Serafima, not wishing to distract the hunter.

"Cobblestones," Serafima said. "They're buried a few inches below the mud. The town should be just ahead." She gestured towards the wall of fog before them.

"Then we move on," Narim said. At his behest, the group plunged deeper into the sweltering valley.

They slogged through the muck for several minutes before the faint silhouette of a wall became visible through the fog. As they drew closer, the valley floor rose and their feet soon fell upon wet cobblestones as the ancient road emerged from the mud. Lucien, still several yards ahead of the others, stopped abruptly after taking a few steps upon the road.

"We've reached the gate," he said.

Narim and the others came to Lucien's side. Before them stood the crumbling archway that had once been the gates of Mournshire.

"By the gods," a mercenary said.

"What happened here, Narim?" Lucien asked.

"You know the legends as well as I, surely," Narim said.

"Well, yes; but they don't tell us much, only that Mournshire was consumed by some nameless evil."

"Are you suggesting I know differently?"

"You knew enough to find Mournshire, and I'm sure your reason for being here is more than curiosity."

"My reasons are none of your concern so long as my coins pay for your blade. Is that entirely clear to you, sell-sword?"

Lucien shrugged and turned to lead the way through the ruined entrance.

The unnatural mist thickened as they passed through the gate but it could not conceal the cadaverous shadows of Mournshire that swelled into view in the distance. Lucien stopped to wait for the others when he reached a small house on the town's outskirts. Moss and lichen covered its wet stone walls and portions of the rotting roof had collapsed.

Narim looked down the long street ahead of them. It was lined with several houses like the one beside them. There was a vague outline of something immense beyond the crumbling homesteads.

"Keep moving," he said.

They followed the winding streets for some time before they come to the town's center. There, amidst the ruins of the ancient stone buildings, they saw a ghastly stone obelisk that welled up from the ground like a disease-ridden tree reaching greedily for the unseen stars far above them. The mist obscured the peak of the unwholesome tower, but its glassy blackish-green surface was sullied with slime and muck. The air around it seemed to pulse with a conscious malevolence.

"What madness is this?" Serafima whispered.

"Behold, the doom of Mournshire," Narim said, momentarily awed by the terrible grandeur of the alien monolith.

"Do you think this wise, Narim?" Serafima asked. "Surely the masters of this foul place watch us even now. What do you hope to gain from this venture apart from a fool's death?"

Narim scowled.

"Might I remind you that I am paying a considerable price for your services? After such a difficult journey, am I to understand that you now intend to turn tail like a coward at the first sign of danger with nary a coin to show for your troubles?"

Serafima's face darkened. Narim could almost see the ways she was considering to strike him dead within her cold, blue eyes. For a moment, he wondered if he had goaded her for the last time. The thought excited him.

"I have no intentions of turning back," she said.

"Come then," Narim said, relishing his victory. "We must make haste."

As Serafima walked away, Ilesha came alongside Narim. She placed her hand on his arm.

"She is wise to fear the darkness that lurks below us," she said. "How can mere mortals possibly comprehend the powers that birthed this foul place? I fear that we should have chosen to remain penniless in Nemdris."

Narim laughed.

"It is the folly of cowards to seek protection in ignorance. Do you fear the shadows so greatly that you would forsake whatever secrets may languish within those primordial walls? Can you not dare to imagine that such knowledge could hold the cosmos itself together or shatter it beyond hope of repair?"

"Such knowledge carries a cost," she said. "That price could well be your soul."

"A pity, for as I have heard it I do not have one to barter. If Mournshire demands a price be paid for its secrets, it shall have to request something else."

"Perhaps it will, Narim of Kurn."

The witch's words lingered in his mind as they approached the vile tower that sprang from the rotten core of Mournshire.

Several inches of swampy water pooled around the base of the massive obelisk and the smell of rotting vegetation hung in the thick, humid air. Tangled strands of vines and weeds hung down over a gaping maw of an archway cut into the tower's side.

It was too dark to see anything beyond the archway until they lit several torches to illuminate the interior of the strange tower. Lucien stepped inside, with the others only a few paces behind him.

They entered an empty room that was as large as the tower's exterior circumference and the walls were made of the same greenish-black stone. In the center was a large circular opening in the floor that had once been sealed off but was now torn open to reveal steps that disappeared into the darkness below. Intense heat welled up through the shattered barricade and the air reeked of decay.

Narim signaled Lucien to continue, and they followed him down the steep, spiraling stairwell. After a descent of several hundred feet the stairs ended in a large chamber that housed two massive doors of black iron, cracked open just wide enough for a large man to slip past. A dull green light of indeterminate origin leaked through the opening, causing the antechamber they stood in to glow faintly.

One by one, they slipped through the doors and beheld the terrible sight beyond them. They stood inside an immense subterranean cavern and in its center rested a monstrous palace even more hideous than the tower hundreds of feet above. Its walls cascaded upwards at strange angles and its twisting, spiraling parapets were mockeries of human architecture. The structure appeared to have been molded into its current form from a single, massive piece of glassy stone. A towering inferno of green flame roared up from the center of the grotesque palace and reached to the cavern ceiling far above.

"There it is!" Narim said, nearly overwhelmed with excitement.

"Gods," Ilesha whispered behind him, her voice filled with a mixture of awe, fear, and, perhaps, love.

"Keep moving," Narim said. "If our fortune holds, the gates will not be sealed."

When they reached the entrance of the palace they found a hole through one of the heavy iron doors that was large enough to walk through.

"Inside," Narim said.

Lucien stepped through the hole and vanished. The darkness swallowed the light of his torch along with the hunter and left everyone staring into the void.

"Lucien?" Serafima said.

There was no answer, not even an echo. It was as if the black air had absorbed her very breath into its being. She looked back to Narim, her face graver than he had ever known it to be.

"We follow," he said.

"Like hell!" a sell-sword shouted. Some of his companions nodded their heads and started backing away from the door.

"No payment's worth this," said another.

"Very well then!" Narim said. "Turn back if you wish, penniless and without honor."

"What good is a bag of coins to a dead man, eh?"

"Aye! I'm going back! Who's coming with me?"

Several more mercenaries walked away from the group until only two remained with Narim, Ilesha, and Serafima.

Narim scowled at the traitors for a moment and then turned to Serafima.

"You choose to remain, eh?"

"Do you think me so without honor that I would abandon a companion in this wicked place?"

"Truly, I am touched by your devotion," Narim said, though he knew she wasn't speaking of him.

Serafima ignored his words. Gripping her broadsword in one hand and a torch in the other, she disappeared through the gash in the iron door.

Ilesha stepped forward and took Narim's hand.

"Come, then," she said. "Let us plunge into the abyss together."

Narim smiled as they slipped inside the shadows, his mind alive with all manner of possibilities laid out before him.

The inky darkness beyond the palace doors was more than a simple by-product of the absence of light. It possessed a physical substance and a dim tinge of awareness that probed dumbly at the strange creatures that stepped into it. The shadows oozed over their bodies like thick tar and pulled them eagerly into its depths. Its meager intellect assailed their minds, desperately seeking some sign or command to obey. But the desires of the shadow went unnoticed, for the strangers wrapped in its dark embrace did not possess the capacity to detect them. Frustrated, the living darkness flung them away as an angry child might toss aside a broken toy, without care for where they might come to rest so long as it was assured a return to the peaceful slumber it had known for so many centuries.

Serafima did not know how long she was enveloped by the foul shadows of the palace before they vomited her onto the smooth stone floor. She coughed, spitting out the thick, black clumps of darkness that had begun to seep into her lungs. Though she felt as if she had nearly drowned, her skin and hair were dry; the only sign of her suffocation being the acrid, shadow-born substance that now slithered back to the looming mass of darkness behind her and the extinguished torch she held in her hand.

The room she had been thrust into was not large, but its high ceilings made it feel relatively spacious. It was dimly lit by glowing gems embedded along the walls at regular intervals and the ceiling towered high above her. Strangely shaped furniture lay strewn about the room; strange because it did not appear to be made for human use. Each piece had too many legs and the seats was shaped in such a way that no man could have sat upon them comfortably. The sickly light of the gems lent an unwholesome appearance to the already alien décor of the room.

Serafima stepped around the scattered furniture, careful not to disturb it in any way. The cold stone beneath her feet shuddered slightly with every step she took and Serafima could not help but wonder if the dark souls of the palace's builders had become trapped within its walls, forever imprisoned by the malevolent will of their foul creation. That the grim palace itself was alive in some way,

Serafima had little doubt. The stone sensed her movements, the shadows watched her, and the stale air tasted the sweat upon her skin.

There was no sign of Lucien, who should have emerged from the darkness only a few moments before her, nor of Narim, who should have been right behind her. After allowing some time to pass, she decided that no one would be stepping through the black void. It was likely, she thought, that they were each standing in a dimly lit room somewhere inside the palace.

Serafima stepped out of the dim room and onto a balcony that overlooked the vast interior of the palace. The mere sight of the chaotic structure stung her eyes and forced her to turn away until her mind adjusted to the madness that sprawled out before her. There was no discernable pattern or design to the staircases, walls, balconies, doors, and halls of the palace; they twisted, turned, and sprang forth from the floors and ceilings as if they were living things with no regard for order or logic. Countless glowing gems identical to those in the room behind her lined the walls, floors, and ceilings of the palace. It was a tangled maze of ornate stone that assailed her senses with fury, a reminder that human eyes were never intended to fall upon such insane configurations of shapes and angles.

She wandered through the labyrinthine corridors and crooked stairways of the ancient, deranged palace for nearly an hour before she found a sign of her companions: The bloody corpse of a humanoid creature that was equal parts ape and salamander lay splayed across the stone floor before her, its hideous, rubbery body riddled with arrows from Lucien's bow. Leading away from the beast was a trail of blood, still wet upon the cold, smooth stone.

Serafima followed the blood through the twisted tangles of hallways until she found Lucien sitting on the stone floor, his back to the wall. He had torn off a strip of his shirt and was using it to bind a wound on his left arm.

"Lucien?"

The hunter started at the sound of her voice, for her approach had been too quiet for even his sensitive ears to detect.

"Serafima!"

"How badly are you hurt?" she asked.

"It isn't too bad, but if I had been any slower that damned thing back there might have taken my arm off."

"Any sign of the others?"

"Nothing. You're the first I've seen."

Serafima nodded.

"We should keep moving," she said.

Together they climbed higher through the spiraling corridors of the palace. Despite their occasional bouts of disorientation they were certain they were moving upward and eventually climbed onto a wide platform that had nothing but a ceiling of solid stone above it. A narrow doorway stood at the far end of the room. It appeared to be the only exit other than the way they had come.

Serafima spotted a pair of bodies that lay on the floor several feet from them and immediately recognized the two mercenaries who had not abandoned them at the gates of the palace. She and Lucien approached the prone figures warily, fearful that they might encounter more of the strange salamander creatures that dwelled there lurking in the shadows.

But as they drew closer it became clear that they had met a far more conventional fate. The hilt of a dagger protruded from the back of one mercenary and the other's throat had been slit. Serafima reached down and pulled the dagger out, then held it out to Lucien. There was no mistaking the distinctively curved, jagged blade. It belonged to Narim.

"That bastard! He's been playing us for fools all along!"

"These two were fools to trust him," Serafima said.

"Look, here," Lucien said, pointing out a trail of smeared blood that led across the floor toward the doorway at the far end of the room. "Neither of them had a chance to draw their blades, so whose blood could this be?"

Serafima remembered that the repugnant creature Lucien killed had shed blood that was thick and black like tar. If the blood did not belong to Narim or the mercenaries, there was only one other possibility.

"The witch."

"Ilesha!" Lucien said. "Narim probably stabbed her before he went for the sell-swords then left her for dead. After he was gone she must have crawled after him, maybe to try to put some manner of curse or hex on him before she bled out."

Serafima nodded, but she had her doubts. It seemed unlikely to her that a killer as precise as Narim would fail to land a lethal strike on an unsuspecting and unprotected woman. And even if he had, why would he leave his dagger behind?

Before Serafima could say anything, Lucien bolted off towards the doorway, following the trail of blood.

"Come on!" he said. "We've got to help her!"

Serafima followed, but she wasn't so sure that letting the witch bleed to death was a bad idea. Duplicitous men like Narim she could at least predict if not fully understand, but there was no way to anticipate the actions of someone like Ilesha, for who could hope to imagine what deviant urges drove those who delved into the black arts of sorcery?

The narrow doorway led outside to the roof of the sunken palace. There they found the source of the green flame they had seen outside the palace. The flames leapt up from a huge altar that was surrounded by alien monuments of stone. Serafima and Lucien stepped outside and followed the smeared blood towards the burning altar.

Remarkably, the tower of flame gave off little heat. They passed under the outer ring of stone monuments and when examined up close they appeared to be some manner of chairs or thrones, for they resembled the strange furniture Serafima had seen upon entering the palace. The burning altar itself was massive, easily as big as any of the stone houses in the ruined town far above them. A series of disturbingly shaped runes adorned the sides of the immense block of stone.

They gave the burning altar a wide berth and circled around to its other side and immediately stopped when they saw what was hidden there. Amidst the queer sculptures of stone surrounding the flame stood a single chair made of metal. It was ornate, with numerous jewels studding its high back and arms, and its familiar shape indicated that it was made for something that was at least humanoid. Two bodies were heaped near the feet of the chair. One of them was covered in dust and its limbs were bent at strange angles. The other Serafima immediately recognized as Narim, even though he lay face down on the cold stone floor. He still wore his black cloak, but it was covered with blood. The trail of blood they had followed ranged all over the area and it was impossible to discern where it ended and Narim's began or if the two were not one and the same.

As they closed in on his motionless form, Serafima succumbed to curiosity and stooped down to examine the other body that lay at the base of the chair. Closer inspection revealed why it appeared so strange from a distance. It looked like the foul creature Lucien had slain, but this one had been dead so long that it little more than a dry husk of brittle bone and leathery skin. A crown of thin iron rods rested upon its skull and crude jewelry adorned its body. Curiously, the withered skin of its left hand had been ripped away from the bone and was crumbled in a pile next to it.

Serafima turned her attention back to Narim.

"Is he alive?" Lucien asked.

"He's still breathing." She reached down and turned him over onto his back and her eyes widened.

Narim's body was covered with cuts and stab wounds, his clothing soaked through with blood. His face was battered, bruised, and split open in places. But his most grievous wound was his left arm, which had been severed at the elbow. Serafima examined the stump closely and became puzzled.

"There is no blood from this wound. It looks like it was burned off. But what could have…"

Narim's remaining hand suddenly shot forward and grasped Serafima by the wrist. His eyes were almost swelled shut, but he forced them open to fix his familiar harsh stare upon her.

"C…couldn't stop her…the witch planned it all…right from the start…" Narim said.

Serafima pried Narim's hand from her wrist and pulled him up to a sitting position, his back leaned against the metal chair.

"Talk," she said.

"It…happened so fast," Narim said. "Ilesha…she caught me by surprise…took my dagger…stabbed me and the others. I… dragged myself out here…tried to stop her…too late…she found it." Narim gestured to the withered creature nearby.

"Found what?" Lucien asked. "This dried out corpse?"

"Not the body, you fool! It was what the...damned thing...wore! A bracer...of the...purest gold...a set of gemstones... flawless ...set within it. Worth...enough to buy your...own kingdom... priceless...perfect...so perfect..."

Narim gurgled and leaned forward to vomit blood into his lap.

"Keep talking," Serafima said.

"...made by the things...they built it...built it all! She knows! She knows!" Narim trailed off as his body shuddered. Serafima tried to shake him back to his senses.

"Knows what, damn you?"

"...gods be cursed...she knows... claws... fire... dark... pain... coming..." he said, clutching feebly at his charred stump of an arm.

And then Narim, the legendary thief of Kurn, died.

Serafima's attempt to make sense of the dying man's last, broken words was cut short when her keen ears picked up a sound behind them. It was the sound of thin, raspy breathing and the scraping of talons upon the smooth stone floor. She looked back and at first thought her eyes deceived her, for it appeared that the shadows on the palace roof were churning like boiling water and swelling towards them. But her vision quickly adjusted and she recognized the dark writhing figures shambling out of the darkness. The horrible forms belonged to the man beasts of the palace, and there were dozens of them.

"Lucien!" Serafima jumped to her feet and readied her broadsword. The creatures spewed forth a chorus of shrieks and charged forward in a mass of fangs and claws.

There was no time for words as the onslaught descended upon them. A few of the monsters paused long enough to rip Narim's body to pieces. Lucien drew his curved saber and slashed desperately as the sea of teeth and talons enveloped them. Serafima dove into the massed ranks of creatures, her heavy broadsword hacking through limbs and splitting skulls with each mighty stroke.

Lucien tried to dart around his assailants, but there was little room for maneuvering and he resorted to swinging blindly at the foul man-things surrounding him. Serafima managed to hold the monsters at bay with crushing blows from her sword as she gave herself over to frenzy. Her feral heart pounded and she bellowed in the throes of her battle lust.

But their courage was of little use, for even as they slew the creatures before them more of the accursed things poured out of the shadows. Serafima's mind was not so clouded with rage that she could not see that their situation was grim. Her mighty limbs would soon tire and her reactions would eventually slow, and when that happened they would be overwhelmed and torn apart. The horde of creatures had nearly surrounded them and it was impossible to reach the door that led back inside the palace.

Serafima could see no hope of escape, but just as she was about to accept the inevitability of death, a slim gap opened in the ranks of the mob and it revealed one of the twisting palace towers that rose just beyond the edge of the roof.

She grasped Lucien's arm and dragged him through the swarming horde of claws towards the tower. The creatures whirled as one and gave chase, trampling over one another in the process and screeching as their prey fled.

"Serafima, what are...?"

"That tower!" She pointed to the twisting spire ahead of them. "We can make it!"

"Are you mad?"

Serafima didn't answer, for as they approached the ledge she saw that she had misjudged the tower's distance from the rooftop. But even if she could have stopped short of the edge, she still would have chanced the jump. A likely death, she thought, was favorable to a certain one. Without hesitation, they flung themselves off the roof.

She immediately realized that their leaps would not carry them across the chasm, but before she had the opportunity to curse her decision, their feet struck something and they landed awkwardly a few feet below the palace roof. Their hands lashed out for support and they steadied themselves on the smooth, stone surface beneath them. Serafima looked down to find they had landed on a lower section of the same twisting tower they had intended to reach. It snaked up from the ground like a crooked tree, twisting and turning so drastically in some places that it nearly doubled back on itself.

"Now what?" Lucien asked.

Serafima looked for a way to get inside the tower but saw no windows or openings. Then she looked up to the roof to see the host of savage beast men staring down, their dark eyes overflowing with malice and murder. Serafima grunted and slid her sword back into its sheath.

"Climb," she said as she thrust herself off the level section of the tower and slid down its smooth surface. Lucien scrambled down the side of the tower behind her just as the vile creatures leapt to the peak of the tower above with ease and crawled down after them.

Their descent was perilous and the smooth stone of the spire offered little in the way of footing. They did not climb so much as slide, fall, and tumble down the length of the bending structure until they reached the ground and sprinted towards the winding passageway that led back up to Mournshire. The bloodthirsty things above, however, clung easily to the stone surface and scampered after them with frightening speed. Neither of them bothered to draw their weapons when they heard the foul horde pour down to the ground and give chase.

The man-beasts closed the distance quickly, but the intruders were far enough ahead to reach the cracked doors safely. Serafima immediately threw herself against the iron door and Lucien joined her. They heard the fanged monsters drawing nearer and as desperation bolstered their strength the heavy door finally moved. Rust broke loose from its ancient hinges and the door finally slammed shut. They heard a locking mechanism click into place somewhere inside it. A thunderous crash echoed throughout the cavern as the horde of beast-things broke against the black iron like waves upon a sea wall.

Before they could rest their weary limbs, a shrill scraping sound pierced their ears. The sound was unbearable and they covered their ears lest their eardrums split. Then the scraping grew louder and faint impressions appeared in the metal door.

"They're clawing through the door!" Lucien said.

"Up the stairs!" Serafima said. The scraping echoed through the stairwell as they fled.

The humid swamp air tasted almost fresh when Serafima and Lucien climbed out of the stairwell and burst forth from the gates of the great obelisk in the center of Mournshire. They had scarcely caught their breath when a familiar but almost forgotten voice greeted them.

"Well, isn't this an unexpected surprise?"

They looked up to see Ilesha standing before them. A pack of the foul man things flanked her, almost cowering in her presence. Her left hand was sheathed in a strange, wiry bracelet that covered her entire forearm and wrapped elegantly around her fingers. Its metal bands were gold and it was crowned with glowing emeralds and ebony gemstones. Something about Ilesha seemed different as well, her eyes were cold and her face betrayed nothing but cruelty and hate.

"Ilesha?" Lucien said.

"Who are you, witch?" Serafima asked.

"I am Ilesha Vanitos Thuria, priestess of Tzaladar."

The mention of the cruel kingdom of Tzaladar made Serafima's lips curl with hatred, for it was the Tzaladarians who slew her father through treachery and still continued to set her countrymen against one another.

"We know what you did to Narim and the others," Lucien said.

"Ah, poor Narim," she said. "He thought he had everything planned so well. The fool! He made my task easier than I dared to hope. There is no greater weakness to be exploited than greed. I must admit, however, that I misjudged your quality. I had hoped my newfound servants would dispose of you, but you seem to have done quite well for yourselves. How interesting. Perhaps I might find a use for you...after you're dead, of course."

Serafima knew her words were no mere idle threat. She was well familiar with the practices of Tzaladar's necromancers.

"What are these creatures?" Serafima asked.

"Why, these are the people of Mournshire. Narim had no comprehension of what occurred here a thousand years ago. The great race that built the city below us possessed knowledge we mortals could only dream of. They built their empires deep beneath the feet of our ancestors. But they saw in us a great potential, for our puny flesh could be easily molded by their sorcery into whatever they so desired.

"Mournshire was their grandest experiment. They sunk the town into the earth and captured all who lived here. Then their sorcery turned the people into the killers you have seen here. But their creations were difficult to control, so they made this." Ilesha held up the strange bracer affixed to her left arm.

"It is attuned to the ever-burning flame below us. The flame is the enduring legacy of the great race, the source of their magical power. This harnesses the power of the flame and bends it to my will. While I wear it, these creatures are mine to command, body, mind, and soul.

"But the creatures revolted against their masters. The strongest among them gained possession of this and used it to destroy their creators. They escaped to the surface, but found that their escape had been in vain, for their bodies could not endure the cold that surrounds this valley. Some of them froze to death trying to escape, but most returned to the palace below. Over the centuries, the creatures degenerated into little more than animals and the truth of their past was lost. Those who now reside here are their descendants.

"But now, with my aid, they can leave Mournshire, and in return they will bring me fortune and glory. Once I learn the secrets of this sorcery no soul will be beyond my power. All will bend to my desires, even the mightiest lords of Tzaladar. A pity you will not live to see my glorious ascension."

Ilesha turned away.

"Kill them," she said.

At the sound of her voice, the pack of creatures charged forward. Ilesha disappeared into the mist, as if the outcome of the battle was already a foregone conclusion.

Serafima and Lucien reacted instinctively, as only years of experience in battle can teach. Serafima crushed the skull of the first to reach them and Lucien skilfully hewed another. There were more than a dozen of the things, but the two companions had no intention of backing down. Their ferocity unnerved the creatures as they hacked and cut their way through them. For the first time in their lives, the beasts felt fear and they faltered, but Serafima and Lucien showed no mercy. They stormed through the mob, leaving only a trail of mutilated, inhuman corpses in their wake as they charged through the foggy ruins of Mournshire in pursuit of the Tzaldarian witch.

Ilesha did not get far before Serafima overtook her. The barbarian lunged for her with blow that would have cloven the witch from shoulder to midsection had she not sprung aside. Ilesha recovered her balance quickly and grabbed Serafima's leg with the jeweled bracer. Intense pain lashed through the limb and it gave out, sending her splashing into the mud. Ilesha drew her dagger and would have driven it into the back of Serafima's neck had Lucien not charged out of the mist just then. His blade cut nothing but air as she slipped away from his weapon's edge and darted out of his reach.

"That will be quite enough of your meddling!" She pointed her jeweled bracer at Lucien and smiled as green fire lashed out from the ancient device.

Lucien threw his hands up in a desperate but puny act of defense as the sickly flame washed over him like a venomous liquid and melted the skin away from his bones. His exposed skeleton turned black and crumbled into ash that was eagerly consumed by the baleful flames. Ilesha laughed, drowning in the sick satisfaction of her newfound power.

As the last remains of Lucien's body were scorched away by the sorcerous fire, Serafima sprang to her feet and attacked. Ilesha's expression of perverse pleasure gave way to shock as Serafima's sword cut through metal, flesh, and bone to sever her arm a few inches above the wrist. A sharp crackle of lightning snapped through the air as the metal blade cut through the golden bracer.

Ilesha staggered back shrieking and dropped to her knees, holding the bloody wound close to her body. Serafima looked down at the piece of the bracer still wrapped around the witch's severed forearm. The jewels within it faded and then crumbled into a grey dust that sank into the thick mud of the swamp.

Suddenly the earth beneath them trembled and nearly threw Serafima to the ground.

"What was that?"

"The palace," Ilesha said. "The breaking must have disrupted the flame below; without its power the palace will collapse!"

"And bring Mournshire down on top of it," Serafima said.

"You've doomed us both, you fool!"

The ground shook a second time and a familiar sound drifted out from the fog behind them.

"The children of Mournshire come..." the witch said.

Her eyes widened.

"I no longer have control over them! They'll tear us apart!"

Serafima looked at the pile of ash and melted flesh that had recently been Lucien. She then glared down at Ilesha, her blue eyes alive with loathing.

"A better fate than you deserve, witch."

Serafima broke into a sprint towards the path of thorns that led out of that fetid valley of sorrow. She didn't look back.

As she raced through the ruins of Mournshire the tremors grew more intense. By the time Serafima reached the town wall, the earth was beginning to split open in places and she could hear the rabid creatures behind her drawing closer. She could scarcely keep her balance when she finally spotted the thorny path that led up to the surface and scrambled up into the thick fog.

Then the earth beneath her fell away and the path of thorns started unraveling. Serafima ran, crawled, and climbed upwards, hoping to stay ahead of the abyss that was opening below. The sounds of pursuit ceased abruptly as she at last cleared the fog and its absence spurred her to quicken her pace. She jumped to grasp a strand of thorns dangling over the edge of the valley as the path disintegrated. The thorns cut into her hands but they held her weight as she hung staring into the abyss below.

Serafima managed to pull herself up to the snowy ground above and lay there motionless for several minutes before hauling her weary body to its feet. She took one long, final look at the ugly gash in the earth and thought of Lucien, who among those who died that day least deserved it. But most of all she cursed the Tzaladarians, who seemed incapable of resisting the temptations of dark powers and knowledge that were better left buried with the dead worlds they had destroyed.

Then Serafima of Rostogov turned her back on the valley of Mournshire. She hoped that her memories of its depths would fade from her mind as quickly as it faded from her sight.

The Path Less Travelled

by Charlotte Bond

The rushes on the floor were old and matted, the air smelt of stale beer, and wood-smoke visibly curled and eddied between the thick, dark oak beams of the ceiling. Richard was sitting brooding in the firelight, empty tables around him, a full tankard in front of him. He was a tall, well-built man with a strong jaw-line, heavy black brows and equally thick dark hair which curled just above his brown eyes. He was contemplating what he was going to do next, idly watching a spider exploring the debris on his table in fits and starts. Richard's mood matched his dark surroundings.

'Sir Richard Beaufort?' said a voice in front of him. Richard looked up, his free hand instinctively going for his sword hilt. The first thing he saw was the charming smile, then the chiselled features that only came with nobility. The stranger had sleek chestnut hair which was gathered back into a short ponytail, strikingly blue eyes and pale and flawless skin unlike Richard's sunburnt and scarred visage. He sat down opposite, still smiling and leaning forward conspiratorially, his hands folded in plain sight in front of him. The stranger was waiting for him to speak, ask his business, so instead Richard slowly raised the tankard to his lips, took a deep draught then lowered it in silence, never breaking his gaze. The stranger still smiled, still waited, and behind his bravado Richard began to feel uncomfortable.

'You know, if left long enough,' the stranger said, gesturing to the spider on the table, 'it will run out of web, rip its own intestines out and start spinning with those in an effort to escape me.' Richard glanced down and grimaced: the spider had stopped its exploration and was trying to weave a little cocoon around itself for protection.

'You must be a mage then,' Richard said bitterly. The stranger's smile widened slightly.

'I see our reputation precedes us,' he replied.

'No, just your cruelty,' Richard said, trying not to show his growing dislike of his new companion. The stranger held out a hand, smooth and unblemished by calluses or any signs of physical labour. The nails were trimmed short and neat and Richard noticed the runes which were permanently scored into the underside of his fingers.

'Guy Trevellyan, at your service,' the stranger said. Richard swore under his breath but had no choice but to reach out and shake the proffered hand. Insulting a Trevellyan was a death sentence; insulting a mage was a fate worse than death.

'With such credentials,' Richard growled, 'you can hardly expect me to believe that you are at my service.'

'I was hoping we could be mutually beneficial,' replied Guy, apparently absent-mindedly tracing a pattern on the table. 'I saw your last tournament,' Guy continued, looking up at him meaningfully. 'Unfortunate about your horse losing a shoe like that.' Richard's tankard froze halfway to his lips. 'Just like the loose saddle which unseated you at Valmond, and the fault in your armour which caused you that nasty injury at Turren.' Richard's knuckles turned white as he gripped his drink.

'A series of accidents,' he growled, trying to keep his voice controlled. Guy shrugged unconcernedly. 'The consequences are the same – you cannot fight in tournaments any more. You lost your horse to Sir Leonard, you have no finance, no support, and just how much do you owe Sir Beric?' Richard was stiff with mute resentment.

'What exactly do you want?' he asked irritably thumping his tankard on the table. 'And can't you stop that?' he added, gesturing to the frantic spider. 'You proved your point and I'm not in the habit of being entertained by cruelty.' It was a dangerous remark – mages were notoriously offended by bluntness so it was with no small amount of surprise that he watched Guy reach out and wave a hand over the bundle so that the frantic movement within it ceased. Guy then delicately plucked the web from the table and tucked it into a pocket.

'I didn't mean for you to kill it,' mumbled Richard.

'Oh don't fret, I haven't harmed it,' Guy replied in a voice you might use to sooth a child. 'I have a much better use for him.' Richard wondered if it might not have been better to kill it.

'And don't think I didn't notice you avoiding my questions – how much do you owe Lord Beric?'

'The exact amount escapes me,' Richard said hesitantly.

'Well, let me remind you – three thousand eight hundred and sixty sovereigns. A lot of money to repay when you have none.'

Richard bristled, clenching and unclenching his sword hand with the tension. 'I'll manage,' he said defensively.

Guy raised an eyebrow quizzically. 'I understand that if you can't pay, Lord Beric has a more… creative way for you to repay the debt.'

Anger flashed behind Richard's eyes as did the image of a multicoloured tunic, bells and ribbons edging the sleeves and hem. Old blood hated new money and Beric had always resented his rise to fame – he'd been only too eager to lend Richard money in his destitution and now he would take Richard's pride and dignity in sorry payment. The thought of his planned servitude and humiliation left a taste of bile in Richard's mouth.

'Jouster to jester in one fell swoop,' Guy added then laughed at his own joke.

'Why do you care what I owe Beric?' asked Richard in a low, dangerous voice.

Guy's face was instantly serious and equally threatening. 'Because I have bought the whole debt off him,' he replied, watching with satisfaction as the surprise spread across Richard's face. 'And I have a much better way for you to discharge your debt. We leave tomorrow.'

Richard's mistrust of the mage did not fade over the coming days of travel. Potent magic ran in a Trevellyan's blood yet Guy acted with such uncharacteristic joviality for a mage that it was disconcerting. He was like no mage Richard had ever met and he could not decide whether that made him more or less comfortable in Guy's company.

In one feature he was a typical mage: he loved the sound of his own voice and spent many hours educating Richard as to the various plants growing next to the road. Since no harm ever came of listening Richard allowed him to continue until his head was spinning with names, cures and curses. The only thing Guy had not told him was where they were going and although Richard had soon stopped asking, it continued to prey on his mind.

127

Early in the afternoon of the third day they passed a small stone obelisk by the roadside; in the heat of the day, the blood offerings were congealed and crusty. Guy stopped and looked at Richard expectantly.

'What?' asked Richard, knowing where this was leading.

'Don't you want to say a prayer to Cruor?' he asked. Richard scowled and walked on.

'I don't pray to Cruor,' he said as dismissively as he could. Richard almost jumped when Guy reappeared at his elbow. He was disturbingly sneaky, even for a mage.

'But Cruor is the blood god of warriors,' Guy said in mild yet genuine surprise. 'Every warrior prays to him. You haven't renounced the gods, have you?' An edge of uneasiness crept into his voice. 'Even we arrogant mages respect them.'

'Of course I pray to the gods,' said Richard testily, refusing to rise to the bait. He quickened his pace but Guy matched it effortlessly. 'I just don't pray to Cruor.'

'But you're a warrior,' said Guy. Richard tried to ignore him. 'Who do you pray to then?' Guy asked. *It's like trying to talk to a stubborn child*, thought Richard. 'Who?' he persisted. 'Who do you pray to, Richard?' Richard stopped dead in the road and stared Guy straight in the eye.

'To Scurra,' he said in a low, dangerous voice, daring Guy to mock the choice. A slight smile twitched the edge of Guy's lips but other than that his face remained impassive.

'You pray to the god of fools and blind luck?' Guy asked, his voice neutral. 'No wonder you were resented by the other warriors,' he grinned before walking away. Richard drew breath for a retort but thought better of it and simply waited a few moments before following.

The road was not an unpleasant one to travel and in the shade of the trees which lined it, the air was filled with the scent of blossom and the sound of buzzing insects.

'So, don't you want to know where we're going?' asked Guy conversationally as they walked along in the cool evening air. Richard had been feeling almost relaxed in the ambient surroundings, but he felt the hairs on the back of his neck begin to prickle at Guy's insolence. Two could play at this game.

'We're going east, aren't we?' he replied in as innocent a voice as he could manage. Guy gave him a mischievous grin.

'That's right, east to the Vale of Edrith,' said Guy. Richard's breath caught in his throat and he almost stumbled. He stopped and stared at Guy who met his glare evenly.

'Why are we going there?' Richard asked tentatively. 'It's cursed.'

'That's right,' replied Guy taking a step closer to him: his posture was casual but his eyes were intent. 'A good curse is always put on a place when you want to keep people away - usually when you want to hide something. In fact,' he added, taking another step closer but Richard raised his hand and took two steps back.

'No,' he said firmly. 'I'm not going anywhere cursed by your lot – there can be nothing hidden in that valley worth that kind of death.'

Guy regarded him for a moment, evidently thinking, but he did not reply. Instead he turned and walked off the path and into the woods. As he disappeared into the undergrowth, Richard swore under his breath. *What's the point in standing here considering my options*, he thought, *when I don't have any.*

Richard trudged back to the campsite in the blood-red sunset, weary and empty-handed.

'I couldn't find any game,' he began to say then stared in surprise at the campsite where he saw Guy crouching next to a merry fire, heartily tucking into a rabbit on a short spit; a second one rested sizzling at the edge of the fire. Guy looked up at Richard's words, juices running down his chin as he gave him a friendly smile.

'Here,' he said, gesturing to the second rabbit, 'yours is still hot, I took them out of the fire before they burned.'

Hunger washed over Richard and his stomach ached with emptiness as he sat down next to Guy, picked up his own rabbit and bit into it deeply. The roasted meat burnt the roof of his mouth but his tongue tingled with honey and spices. He chewed slowly, suspiciously, glancing at Guy who caught his gaze and shrugged casually.

'Being a mage means being good at herbs,' he said. 'And knowing your herbs has the benefit of being bloody good at cooking.

Do you like it?' Richard nodded reluctantly and Guy smiled again in apparent pleasure.

'I can't believe I'm eating a meal prepared by a mage,' Richard muttered quietly but not quietly enough.

'Against your principles, is it?' asked Guy. His voice was controlled but cold and tinged with anger. Richard froze mid-bite but it was too late to take his words back. 'Ungrateful *and* cynical,' Guy added, his voice like ice. Richard could feel the pressure of magic making his head throb and he thought he might vomit his meal straight back up. 'Remember, *Sir* Richard,' Guy spat his title with derision 'you may be able to slice my head off with that clumsy sword of yours but I could just as soon crush every bone in your body without even breaking your skin.' Richard's head swam with pain as the magic flowed around him, he could barely breathe. 'As it is,' Guy continued then paused and suddenly the pressure ceased. Richard gulped air down gratefully then looked back at Guy who was regarding him with a strange mixture of resentment and vulnerability. 'As it is, I need you, Sir Richard.'

There was an uneasy silence; Richard was thinking of all the horrific injuries a mage recently inflicted on the king when it was suggested that he needed the king more than the other way round. He could feel the magic that still hung in the air and wisely kept silent.

'If it makes you feel any better,' said Guy, returning to his meal, 'you're not strictly eating with a mage because I'm not a mage anymore. They threw me out.' The air was suddenly colder and Richard considered this piece of information. He knew Guy's volatile mood hung on his answer so he chose his next words very carefully.

'You mean, not only have I got myself involved with a mage, I've got one that even the other mages don't want?' Guy's eyes narrowed instantly and it took all of Richard's mental effort to get his grin just right – teasing, charming and just like Guy's. He held his breath, praying that his gamble would pay out. Guy regarded him for a moment then grinned himself and held out his hand.

'Two outcasts together?' he asked with that familiar joviality. Richard exhaled with relief and as he took the proffered hand he felt his fingers tingle at the magic which flowed through Guy's touch. Richard marvelled at what it must feel like to have magic flowing through you all the time: no wonder so many mages went mad.

As the journey continued, they met fewer travellers on the road so that it was deserted as they approached their destination. It soon turned into a stony track with overgrown plants invading it at every opportunity.

'It's the magic that surrounds this place,' explained Guy as Richard tried to hack a passage through the undergrowth with his sword.

'If it's magic,' Richard had grumbled, 'can't you do something about it?' Guy had merely smiled at that and Richard had continued until the weeds clawing at his chest finally gave way to lush open meadow. Guy took a deep breath, letting it out slow and controlled.

'We're here,' he said softly. Richard looked around him. They were at the bottom of a valley, the hills like green walls, the wood respectfully edging the valley floor and in the middle stood the remains of a stone cottage.

'It doesn't look cursed to me,' said Richard.

'What did you expect?' asked Guy mischievously. 'A barren wasteland?'

'Well, yes actually,' shrugged Richard. He had reluctantly begun to warm to Guy. His exuberant attitude, at first so irritating, had distracted him from the danger and magic which seemed to press closer with every step. Guy began to wade through the waist-deep grass towards the cottage and Richard followed.

'All nature will cluster around magic. This place is overflowing with power – can't you feel it?' asked Guy.

'A little,' Richard admitted.

'Do you know how this place was cursed?' called Guy as they stumbled towards the cottage.

'I heard something about a coven of witches,' replied Richard distractedly as he fought with a thistle. 'Became too powerful, called up something unpleasant and it destroyed them.' Guy barked out a laugh.

'I love folklore,' he said. 'It's fascinating to see truth twisted beyond plausibility. There was a coven of witches, they were very powerful and they did attract unwanted attention, but of a human not demonic sort. And they weren't destroyed, they're still here.' Richard stopped dead and Guy grinned at him mischievously. 'Don't worry,' he continued, 'you're perfectly safe for now.'

At Guy's instruction they searched the remnants of the cottage and having moved a small avalanche of stones from the crumbling fireplace, Richard discovered an opening which dropped down into a tunnel. Guy crouched next to him, surveying the darkness with a frown.

Richard looked at the mage and saw the determination on his face; dark circles under his eyes gave him a haggard appearance.

'Why did they kick you out?' Richard asked tentatively. Guy looked up, disturbed from his reflections. There was no mischievous smile or enigmatic answer.

'I found something,' he replied. 'Something which has been hidden for millennia. I didn't even know what I had found but someone noticed their secret had been uncovered. I didn't get so much kicked out as fled for my life.'

'So what's down there then?' Richard asked slightly nervously. Guy's eyes gleamed with promise.

'A weapon,' he replied in a low whisper then his frown deepened and he avoided Richard's gaze. 'When I start down that tunnel I shall probably be a dead man. I have no kin to continue my debt so you can go home.' Guy swung his legs into the opening and dropped down, disappearing into blackness, leaving Richard suddenly alone with a dilemma.

Richard looked around the meadow then contemplated the tunnel again. Was there anything waiting for him back in Riversedge that was worth the long walk back? He had never met a mage who gave you a choice before, one who had flashes of humanity streaking through his power. But then again, he had a life he could salvage back in the city. There was no reason to follow Guy into that tunnel.

No wonder I pray to the god of fools, he thought angrily before jumping down into the passageway.

Richard's eyes took a few moments to adjust to the darkness but the first thing he saw was Guy's white teeth, revealed in a smile of relief. The mage plunged ahead with confidence but Richard had to guide himself tentatively in the dimness; he found the tunnel was narrow enough that he could extend both arms out to the sides and feel his way along both walls at once. The passage was not completely pitch black since a sickly light changed the darkness into gloom. Richard looked in vain for the source but it seemed to be seeping out of the walls themselves. The tunnel sloped gently downwards and as they went deeper the fresh air turned stale and walls became harder, more compact earth.

'Come on, Richard! Don't be so slow!' called out Guy as he disappeared into the dimness ahead. Cursing under his breath, Richard picked up the pace but had barely taken more than ten strides when he ran straight into the back of Guy and both of them toppled forward. Richard braced himself for the impact of earth but none came, he simply kept falling. Guy was clutching onto him with a fierce grip.

'You fool!' hissed Guy, 'you've knocked us both into a pit.'

'I wasn't the idiot standing in the dark, at the edge of a chasm, not telling his companion that there's a bloody great hole in front of them.'

After the bursts of anger there was only silence and the air rushing past their ears as they fell.

'Why haven't we hit the ground yet? How deep is this hole?' Richard asked.

'I didn't say it was a hole,' Guy replied, 'I said it was a pit. A bottomless pit to be precise.' Richard took another moment of silence to consider this. He kept expecting the impact of ground to prove Guy wrong.

'Really?' he said eventually, feeling it was an inadequate response in the circumstances. He could feel Guy nodding. 'What do we do then?'

'We'll just have to wait,' said Guy in far too much of a matter-of-fact voice for the situation.

'Wait?' Richard asked disbelieving.

'Yes, and don't let go,' added Guy.

It seemed like they had been falling for hours and as no bone-breaking ground rushed to meet them, Richard had reluctantly accepted Guy's explanation.

133

'I can't feel my feet anymore,' he whispered, but Guy rebuked him into silence. Richard could hear nothing but the rushing air and his own heartbeat.

'Give me your sword,' whispered Guy urgently. 'Quickly. But don't let go.' Richard clumsily unsheathed his sword and handed it to Guy. 'Good,' Guy said. 'Now, I'm going to let go of you. I want you to grip onto my waist, wrap your arms all the way round and brace yourself.'

'What the –' Richard began but Guy cut him off sharply.

'Do it!' he hissed forcefully and Richard obeyed. He heard Guy mutter a spell, felt his muscles tense and then a sudden jolt which was so violent it nearly broke Richard's grip on the mage. They had stopped and were just dangling in mid-air.

'Try and climb up me and onto the ledge,' said Guy through gritted teeth. 'Do it, quickly,' he hissed when Richard protested. Despite the danger, Richard felt ridiculous as he began to clamber over and around Guy towards the sword he was clinging onto. Richard reached out to grip the hilt and felt the warmth of it flow through his fingertips: only something that had been charmed felt that way.

Richard stretched out his other hand and was surprised to touch stone – his sword was buried almost up to its hilt in solid rock. Richard could now see a ridge above them and dim light beyond. He secured a handhold and heaved himself back onto the path before reaching over to help Guy.

The mage sank back against the rock, panting and trying to rub the burning out of his arm muscles.

'What in the hells just happened?' asked Richard. Guy focussed bleary eyes on him and gave a weak smile.

'That was the first trap, the test of Earth, my friend,' he replied. 'We still have Air, Water and Fire to go.' Guy eased himself to the edge of the chasm and tentatively leaned over, muttered a charm under his breath and the sword slid free of rock. He returned it to Richard.

'Felt more like a test of Air to me,' mumbled Richard.

'That's why I'm the mage and you're not,' said Guy as he got up unsteadily.

'Where exactly are we?' asked Richard.

'Back where we started,' replied Guy. He gestured across to the chasm. 'Look – that's the ledge where you careered into me.' Guy continued as they headed along the path once more. 'You see, a bottomless pit isn't really that. It's more a kind of…circle.'

'A circle?' said Richard dubiously.

'We fell through the floor, through the rock, out through the ceiling, down through the floor again, without even realising it. It's an endless loop from which many have failed ever to escape.'

Implausible nonsense, Richard thought but asked out-loud: 'What are the other tests then?'

'I'm not exactly sure,' said Guy. Richard raised an eyebrow in the gloom and Guy added 'but I have a good idea.'

'Comforting,' muttered Richard and they continued on in silence. The path continued to slope down and they walked until Richard's legs burned with the effort.

Suddenly Guy stopped and held up a hand for Richard to do the same. Richard looked past the mage's shoulder and saw that they were standing before an arch in the passageway.

The arch looked out of place – smooth white marble, surprisingly free from dirt for its underground location. Richard's gaze travelled up and he saw intricate runes carved into the apex. Guy was looking at them too, frowning and whispering something in a tongue Richard did not recognise.

'What does it say, Guy?' The mage's frown deepened then vanished.

'I haven't a clue,' he said cheerfully. Richard stared at him aghast but Guy just grinned cheekily and moved forward to peer into the room beyond the arch, careful never to pass underneath it.

'Well, do you at least know what is in there?' asked Richard irritably.

'Nothing,' replied Guy. 'The room is empty.'

'Good, then let's go,' said Richard heading towards the arch. Guy turned and blocked the way.

'How in the hells did you manage to survive so long being so stupid?' he asked in a flush of anger but he quickly backed down and rubbed his forehead in tiredness. 'In a place built by mages, hidden by mages, riddled with traps and designed to hold the deadliest of weapons, aren't you suspicious of a room which is apparently harmless?' he asked in a weary voice. Richard thought for a moment.

'The test of Air?' he ventured. Guy looked at him in surprise then beamed.

'Excellent!' Guy exclaimed and fished into his pocket to produce a palm-sized ivory box. Richard watched him curiously as he knelt on the floor, opened the box and shook out the contents. A dozen silvery spiders tumbled onto the floor in a pile and Guy shooed them towards the archway with whispered words. Richard had thought they might have vanished from sight but their little bodies shone with a silvery light as they scurried about.

'Do I want to know what you're up to?' asked Richard, watching the spiders in fascination as they began to weave webs which also shimmered in the dark.

'I don't know, do you?' asked Guy, leaning back against the wall, taking out a pipe and beginning to smoke casually.

'Yes, I want to know. What is it they say? "Knowledge is power".' Guy looked at him with astonishment then shrugged amiably.

'Fine. You were right, it's a test of Air. There is nothing in that room except air but not the sort you breathe in and out. It is alive in its own right and it's always hungry. There is a path through it but if you stray, you get caught like a fly in a spider's web.' Guy smiled at the irony of his solution. 'I trained my own little spiders to find the path and weave it out for us. So long as we don't break the webs and follow the path they make, we should be fine. But for now we just have to wait.'

It could have been as much as a whole day later by the time Guy decided it was safe to progress. The hours had given Richard ample time to consider all the horrors which might lurk within the dark room and his usually sensible nature had been overcome with nerves.

Their progress was tortuously slow. The hairs on the back of Richard's neck prickled painfully and he was breathing heavily but Guy refused to go any faster. The path snaked around the room, at times crossing itself and it was so narrow in places that Richard could feel the webs brushing against his arms. At one turn Richard found himself staring directly into the eye socket of a brown, grinning skull which peered out from the darkness beyond the shining webs. Such was the shock that Richard nearly stepped backwards and it was only the sudden restraining hand of Guy which saved him from breaking through the webbed-wall behind him.

'Careful,' Guy warned in a strained whisper before they moved on. All of Richard's muscles were aching with tension, he could feel exhaustion creeping over him and it was with immense relief that he stepped out through the arch on the other side of the room. Guy was already collapsed on the floor, equally exhausted but he managed a weak grin.

'Halfway there,' he said. Richard slumped on the floor next to Guy and produced a leather-bound flask from which he took a long draught. Guy looked at him curiously when offered it and it was Richard's turn to smile.

'My own particular potion,' he explained. 'Homemade.' Guy took the flask and spluttered at the first mouthful. He peered suspiciously into the container, wrinkled his nose at the alcohol haze which leaked from it then took a second, deep draught.

When they had recovered their strength they started down the corridor again; the floor was still sloping and Richard wondered just how far underground they were.

For another hour they trudged along the passage, forced for much of it to go hunched under the low ceiling. The air was getting stale and thin when they turned a corner and Richard saw a pale blue light ahead of them. The passageway opened out into a high vaulted cave, blue crystals sparkling on every wall emitting the strange light. Richard gazed in awe round the cave which must have been half a mile across, and he could just see the exit on the other side of a shallow lake which lapped at his feet. Guy started to wade into it and Richard followed.

'Test of Water?' he asked and the mage nodded, concentrating.

'Keep your wits about you,' Guy said.

The water was warm and soon up to waist height so Richard had to carry his sword across his shoulder. The surface reflected the sparkling crystals almost hypnotically.

Not a particularly unpleasant Test, he thought. It reminded him of the time he had spent at the bathhouse in Allon. He had been exhausted that time too and had welcomed being enveloped in warm water, breathing exotic perfumes through the steam. Knights always attracted attention, especially those who had just won the city tournament so there had been no shortage of bathing attendants to massage his aching leg muscles and soothe his painful shoulders. He recalled one particularly striking raven-haired woman who would run her fingers through his hair, sluicing it with water and oils while all he would do was close his eyes, lean back and relax.

When the water rushed into his lungs, Richard came out of his reverie with shock. He was submerged in the underground lake, being dragged under the water by hands which were not young and delicate but grey, bloated talons which kept a vice-like grip on his limbs. Thin black hair billowed in front of his face and Richard turned to stare at an eyeless corpse; what was left of her skin clung to her skeleton like algae and her hand was fastened securely on his shoulder. She was one of many and his scream was a torrent of bubbles as he thrashed helplessly.

Suddenly the grip on his left ankle vanished and he was able to kick frantically with his free leg. Then the hands tugging on his left shoulder were ripped away and Guy hauled the free half of him out of the water. Richard had managed to hold onto his sword and now he sliced at the creatures around them in the water but the sword passed freely through them as if they were made of water themselves. He could feel more hands gripping his legs, trying to pull him back down.

'Here, use this,' called Guy over the sound of thrashing water. He handed Richard a cane which matched the one he was sluicing through the water. Richard ignored it and kept striking at the creatures with his sword in panic. 'Use it!' commanded Guy and Richard thrust the cane down through the water in anger towards his ankles. He stumbled in amazement as the bony hands released him at the touch of the wood.

'What are they?' asked Richard, still spluttering with the residual water in his lungs.

'Remember I said that coven of witches was not destroyed but still haunted the site?' said Guy. He did not need to finish his explanation; Richard looked at the watery shadows which circled around them and shivered.

'So why are we swotting at them with sticks?' he asked, his ragged breathing gradually returning to normal.

'These switches are made from elder.'

'So?'

'So, elder trees are renowned for acting as prisons for witches,' said Guy. 'These switches act as wards against them, although if I were them I don't know whether I'd prefer endless imprisonment in a tree to a damned existence down here.'

They had not been even halfway across the lake when the creatures had struck so they had to finish their journey warily. Although the dark shapes swarmed around them, occasionally brushing against them, the elder seemed to keep them at bay and Richard was glad to feel dry ground underneath him again.

'They can't reach us on the bank, can they?' he asked. Guy shook his head.

'No, they're bound to the water,' he replied. They went a little way down the passage to rest and dry out. Richard stared wearily back down the passage to the sparkling cave.

'That'll be a story to tell,' he said idly, 'beating off water-witches with a piece of wood.' Guy laughed amiably and it sounded strange in this dark, depressing place.

'I promise you the next Test will make a better story,' he said, 'and you will have a larger role in it too.' Richard tensed but Guy refused to elaborate.

Richard's muscles were even stiffer when he got up yet he was pleased to be moving. They walked in silence again for a while, Guy in the lead, his shoulders hunched despite the higher ceiling.

'If you're right, the next test is one of Fire,' he said, 'and I don't understand how I can fight it when you can't.' Guy stopped suddenly at turn in the tunnel, held a finger to his lips then beckoned Richard forward.

'I thought that's what knights fought,' he whispered and leaned back against the wall so Richard could peer around him at what lay beyond.

The passage widened out into a cave here too, but this one was much smaller than the crystal cave and its wall were blackened and cracked. At least six men could easily have walked abreast

139

through it but curled up in the middle was the reason why none would dare.

'A dragon!' breathed Richard in wonderment. Dragons had not been seen for centuries and even now he could not believe the sight but his initial awe faded as he looked closer. The dragon's scales were a deep rich green, flecked with red so that it shimmered and changed colour just by breathing, but patches were missing and the skin underneath was puckered with old wounds. As it lay a little on its side, Richard could see that it was not scaled all over but had course, wiry hair on its throat and belly which was matted with dirt and blood, bald where a large scar ran from its shoulder. Richard listened to its breathing which was irregular and laboured.

'Don't be fooled by its appearance,' Guy said, 'however old it may look, it's still a killer.'

'A killer?' said Richard. 'Isn't that what you're trying to make me into?' Yet he could not deny the rush of excitement that was building in him – no knight in his generation could claim to have fought a dragon.

'Well, what do we do?' asked Guy. Richard looked at him in surprise: he had never heard of a mage asking for instructions and he was lost for ideas.

'May as well try and see if we can sneak past it,' replied Richard. 'No sense in wasting energy fighting it if we don't have to.'

'Less of this "we" business,' said Guy. 'Dragons are impervious to magic so there's little I can do. That's why it's the final test – someone highly skilled in magic can get through the first three tests but anyone who has spent their time learning magic to that degree has never taken the time to master a sword. It's impossible to devote your life to both arts.' When Richard looked dubious he added: 'Have you ever heard of a warrior mage?' Richard had to admit that he had not. He took a deep breath and stepped out into the cave.

A rush of fire nearly engulfed him before he had time to dive to the floor where he had to roll to avoid a scaly forearm which tried to crush him into the sand, then another one aimed at his head but then he rolled straight into the beast's back leg which sent him skidding across the floor and crashing against the wall with one kick.

He barely had the strength to avoid the second rush of fire but his heart beat faster with the thrill of combat.

Richard pulled out his sword and stood ready to advance. He expected another rush of fire but the dragon merely sat on his haunches, watching him.

It's defending, not attacking, thought Richard and he advanced cautiously. The dragon opened its mouth to vomit fire again but disgorged only heat haze and sulphur which was still deadly enough to singe the clothes on his right arm but as Richard dodged sideways he landed a blow to the dragon's left forearm and the creature stumbled forward with a screech. Its chin hit the ground and blood spurted from its mouth as it bit its tongue in two. Richard used its momentary daze to aim a thrust up and under its forearm. The dragon twitched and whined before it lay still on its side.

Guy hurried straight past Richard as he stood wiping blood and ash from his clothes.

'This way! Quickly!' called the mage enthusiastically.

'You're welcome, and I'm fine, thanks,' grumbled Richard as he pulled his sword free from the beast. He went to wipe the blood off with the end of his tunic and noticed with a cold dread that the dragon's chest still moved as it breathed shallowly.

Slowly, with sword ready and muscles tensed, he moved round to look at its head. Its one good eye stared up at him with a pitifully familiar stare that Richard had seen on men fatally wounded on the battlefield: men in agony, begging mutely for the release of death. Richard was suddenly overwhelmed with sadness as he watched the last dragon in existence wish its life away. The beast's breath wheezed in its lungs and with each exhalation the blood around its mouth bubbled and seeped. He bent over and laid a hand on its head, the way you might comfort a faithful dog, before placing the point of his sword against the beast's throat.

Better than this half-life, he thought sadly and holding its gaze Richard thrust his sword down hard and fast. The beast convulsed once, weakly, and then he saw the life die behind its remaining eye.

With this hollow victory behind him Richard walked heavily into the room beyond which was completely circular with walls of smooth, hard earth arching over the floor in a dome. Set around the walls, equal distances apart, were nine doorways, each appearing to have a numeral carved into its lintel. In the centre was a raised stone altar in front of which Guy was standing; Richard could hear his own footsteps echoing as he approached.

'Don't feel so bad,' Guy said when Richard appeared at his shoulder. He spoke distractedly as he examined something in front of him on the altar. 'Dragons are immortal, their soul gets reborn in another dragon. It will reincarnate in another.'

'In another what?' asked Richard wearily. 'Last I saw there were no other dragons left for it to be reborn into. I just killed the last damned one.' Guy looked up at him and his eyes gleamed, making Richard painfully aware of how little he knew about this magical world he had stumbled into.

Guy turned his attention back to the altar and held something up for Richard to see.

'I've found it,' he whispered reverentially. Richard had expected a magic sword with which to cut down your enemies, a staff of power to smite those who stood in your way, a crystal which could bring healing and wisdom to those who used it.

'It's a book,' Richard said as if the words left a bad taste in his mouth. 'And a tatty one at that. We've come all this way for a book? What kind of a weapon is that?'

'An exceptional one, my friend,' Guy replied as he wrapped their prize in a cloth and slipped it into the bag over his shoulder. 'You said it yourself: knowledge is power.'

'What a shame you will never get to use that power,' sneered an icy voice behind them.

Richard and Guy spun round to see four hooded figures standing before them. Richard guessed they must have appeared from the archways behind them. Each wore a long cloak which hung to the floor with a deep hood to shadow their features and each carried a staff as tall as its owner.

'These look more like the mages I know,' Richard muttered under his breath but Guy ignored him.

The figure who had spoken stood a little in front of the others. He held out a hand.

'Give me the book, young Trevellyan.' Richard's head began to thump as the magical power in the room built exponentially. He glanced at Guy and saw that his face was flushed, strained but determined.

'Do you really think I came all this way just to hand it back?' Guy asked. Richard could hear the tension in his voice even though he strived for his usual joviality. 'You taught me better than that, Master.' The figure gave a low chuckle. Richard saw one of the others tighten his grip on his staff but before Richard could formulate a defence a surge of magic knocked him off his feet, threw him against the altar and nearly crushed the breath out of him. For a few seconds Richard saw Guy resisting but his face was contorted in pain and then with a brief scream it was over. Richard felt the pressure on his chest ease but it took his eyes a few moments to recover from the sea of lights which swam in his vision. Blearily he saw that all four of their attackers were laid out flat on the ground, their staffs scattered or broken under them. Richard felt an overwhelming respect for Guy – four against one was not odds he would have liked even without magic. He crawled over to Guy who was himself lying on the floor, knocked unconscious by the blast of magic.

'Come on, let's go,' hissed Richard, shaking him harder than he meant. 'I don't want to wait around for their next request. Guy? Get up.'

Not unconscious, thought Richard. *Dead. And strangely cold too.* Richard felt a surge of sadness and pity – they had come all this way for nothing. *I hope it wasn't too painful.*

Richard glanced at the others lying on the floor. Their chests moved gently showing they still breathed so Richard did not waste any time. He untangled Guy's bag and hung it from his own shoulder.

Not for nothing, my friend, he thought. *In payment of my debt.* He got up unsteadily and considered his options: nine doors, each one leading somewhere unknown. They had come through the one with the numeral two but there was a bottomless pit and bunch of witches down there. If he was lucky he might be able to outrun the mages when they woke up, but not if he went that way. Quickly and quietly he examined each arch in turn; all had pitch black beyond them, some of them had distant noises – voices, running water, screaming. As he approached numeral nine his senses were accosted by the scent of honeysuckle on a warm breeze. He glanced behind

143

him as one of the mages twitched and then with a deep breath he walked straight through the doorway.

Damn, he thought. *I'm all wet again. At least it's only my boots this time.* He stepped out of the stream and examined his surroundings quickly. He was standing in a clearing in a forest and he could see a road up ahead. He did not even wonder how he had got from an underground cave to a shady glade but he made his way through the undergrowth and looked swiftly around him; the Red Hill was instantly recognisable in the distance and since the sun was on his left that must mean that Riversedge was about five miles away. He was almost back where he had started.

Keeping close to the edge of the road and ducking into the bushes at every sign of company, Richard made his way back to Riversedge and slipped unobserved into the city through the smaller east gate.

He took rooms at The Boaters Inn and did not stop looking behind him until he had a bolted door at his back. Then he would have sat and wept except his exhaustion held back any tears.

Let's see what Guy's life bought him then, he thought as he took the book out of the bag and removed the cloth. The book looked no different from any other he had seen before except there was no title, no indication as to its contents. There was simply a small circle engraved in the leather cover with flecks of gold still embedded in the grooves and a further haphazard engraving in the top left hand corner. Richard's skin tingled when he touched it, the same low level awareness of magic he had felt around Guy, not the chokingly bitter magic that had emanated from his killers.

Does that make it any safer? he wondered. Richard realised he was holding his breath and he exhaled slowly, tensed himself for the horror he was certain would be unleashed and then he opened the book. He coughed and spluttered at the cascade of centuries old dust which erupted in his face. Richard waved a hand to clear the air then looked down at the minute writing which scrawled across each page.

'What language is that?' he muttered to himself. 'I don't understand a single word.'

'You're not alone,' said a voice behind him. 'Nobody alive can read that script any more.' Richard jumped up, the book falling from his hands as he reached for his sword. He knew he had bolted the door from the inside but now it stood wide open and a tall, slender man in a dark brown cloak leaned against it. His elegant features and self-assured stance were strangely familiar.

'My name is Nolan Llywelyn' he said with a slight incline of his head in greeting. 'I'm the brother of Guy Trevellyan. Well, half-brother: we share the same father.'

Richard could not deny the similarities in height and features, and they definitely shared the same arrogance but Guy's words returned to haunt him: *I have no kin to continue my debt.*

'You must be the bastard then,' Richard said with a straight face. Shock turned to a cloud of fury which blackening the mage's face. Richard was taken aback by the difference – where Guy's anger had been fierce, Nolan's was pure malevolence. Richard kept his expression blank, innocent, and shrugged. 'You don't have the Trevellyan name.' Nolan's skilful smile was swift to return. He even had the same ability to oscillate between moods as Guy.

'A misunderstanding,' Nolan said pleasantly. 'And apologies for the hasty introductions but I think you will find I am not the only one interested in that book. But if you come with me, I know someone who can read it for us.' Richard frowned.

'You said no one alive could read that script,' he said warily. Nolan flashed a familiar enigmatic smile.

'Yes, I did,' he replied.

Not for the first time that day, Richard found himself considering his options and suddenly realised he had more than he thought.

1842
Victorian Cadence

The mist is ever present at the docklands, convulsing at the water like a
dying rabid beast,
Ghost-white seagulls hover above as if holding a séance for the deceased.
They say that if you're bewitched by its darkness, hear the melancholy cries
within the spiralling spindrift,
You'll be lost forever to the lonely ocean waters, will forever roll in its
chaotic abyss ...

*

The boy's teeth were chattering hurrocks, as he crouched and shivered at
the wharf;
The horn of the steamship cut through the fog, its distant body a skeleton of
white gauze.
The sky cracked: two globes of fire bounced off the sea, its inky bowels
disturbed by a mutinous presence;
The boy pitched into Triton's cerulean tide – the final chords of his
Victorian cadence.

He trailed to the ocean floor, like liquid-silver, down to the darkest depths
of shining black glass,
And in its mirror he saw her float to him, her hand soft as moonglade
'gainst the arch of his back.
Her breath was kindling to his cadaverous body; the sea bubbled from her
Salome song,
Her scales were electrifying needles; she coiled around him her
smouldering, seductive warmth.

At her golden palace in those tumultuous waters, he combed his fingers through her dishevelled copper hair,
And he made his halcyon mermaid a floating nest of fine-spun coral gossamer.
Phosphorescent fish lamped a serpentine pathway to this love-lair in the pink, scalloped reefs,
He clung to the fluid movements of her flamenco dance, caressed her tiny hands cobwebbed with quartz crystal beads.

As the sun rose so their cavern grew sable, and the colour began to seep from this world;
She slipped the ferryman's penny into his mouth, her tears raining down like salty, splintered pearls.
The shadow of the pier cast an oblong altar, and he drifted soberly into its tomb;
She veiled her eyes with the velvet fronds of her hair; he floated back to the grey docklands' slums.

At dawn they dragged the body from the water, laid him out by the spot from whence he'd leaped,
Like the workhouse clothes he'd left there neatly folded, the young lad's face was worn-out and bleached.
His threadbare breeches still blackened and tainted in spite of their nightlong sea soak,
The boy's chiselled jaw was set high and proud – he wore poverty like a rich, princely cloak.

*

As though through a conch shell he hears the song of the siren, and though his body's key-cold, his heart soars,
His Victorian nightmare has come to an end, the frozen lock of lonely wont has at last thawed.
A silhouette rises from the boy's impoverished body and dives back into the sea;
In life he was unwanted and hungry: in death he is loved and replete.

Carly Dugmore

Elemental Telecommunications by Suryan Philip

Why Stars Are The Way They Are

by Felicity Bloomfield

Missy Myway was the sweetest of the starlets, and her soul was as great as the ocean. Fans were charmed when she wore bunny slippers to her first award ceremony, peeking out from under a designer gown. Her face was as expressive as her music, grinning as her blonde hair fell across one eye, or sweetly calling attention to the successes of her favourite charities. People called her the girl of a thousand smiles.

Her only foible was that she did not like having her picture taken. It was a phobia based on the beliefs of certain third-world cultures that cameras could steal a person's soul. She sat for portraits each day, and passed them out to photographers as gifts, hoping to discourage their professional enthusiasm. They merely photographed her handing out the pictures.

Even as she retreated back into restaurants or behind gates, her sharpest rebuke was to say, 'I don't want my photo taken, you drip.' Young girls began using the word 'drip' as hip new slang referring to anyone wielding a camera.

Missy and her high school sweetheart were married. The drips were greeted cordially by Missy's manager, and invited to leave their cameras at the door and enter. The ceremony was performed in the backyard of Missy's childhood home. Most of the town attended, but they were still outnumbered by photographers, twitching frustrated fingers as Missy sparkled like never before.

As Missy and her husband were permitted by reverent order to kiss, cameras appeared from under seats and inside handbags. The flashes pierced her closed eyes. She broke the kiss and stared around as if caught in a deadly trap. That iconic look of interrupted innocence appeared on the cover of no less than three major magazines within the week.

Something changed in the press that day. They followed Missy in taxis and unmarked vans, taking pictures of her at the beach, with family, and through the windows of her home. Photos appeared of her getting drunk as she sought anonymity by any means. Soon there were pictures of her fighting with her husband,

and both of them trying new and harder drugs. A photo of Missy with a male prostitute made the photographer's career. The prostitute went on to star in a hit reality show. Even in the sealed courtroom, as Missy wrangled with the man who would soon become her ex-husband, someone managed to secretly take photo after photo after photo.

As Missy left the courtroom a hoard of paparazzi caught her on the steps in a blaze of light. She shrieked and swore and swung at the nearest. The drip grabbed at her, and snagged a handful of fabric.

'You want some?' she shrilled. 'Take it!' She tore at the shirt, bursting the buttons, and threw it in his delighted face. Her bra followed, and the respectable skirt she'd worn to court. Famous undies matched the bra on the ground. The flashes were like an electric storm. Missy shielded, not her face or her nakedness, but somewhere near her heart. Soon there was nothing left to take.

Missy Myway was the sweetest of the starlets, and her soul was as great as the ocean. Even the ocean can be emptied, drip by drip.

Diamond Throne by Suryan Philip

The Hurl and the Stone Rose

by Perry Mc Daid

Slieve Mish Mountains played *headie* with the glowering clouds, seeming to bounce their burgeoning mass off each consecutive peak as Cathbad's small craft skimmed the restive waters of Dingle Bay. It was that time of the year again, and he was the last true druid.

A frown fleetingly marred his handsome features as he reflected upon how the primitives had bastardised the essence of true druidry, using its tradition and presumption of authority to perpetuate their own warped superstitions. It had been right to drive them out of Ireland: worshippers of serpent's eggs were not given to clear thinking, certainly not qualified to be handing down religious or judicial edicts.

His own people had retreated into the hidden kingdom, only to be forced to relocate again and again by the blind plague the primitives named progress. Finally they had had to integrate into a society the rules and point of which were beyond them.

His attention was drawn back to the present: The Talon, a geographical feature which spanned the inner bay, guarding the approach to his destination with deceptive readings and treacherous currents. He smiled. The Golden Torque would not be surprised by any trick of the sea or land. The little craft negotiated the combined fortifications with ease, weaving in and out between the ancient spells which supplemented the natural barriers afforded by The Talon.

Spotting a figure on the strand, Cathbad reached out with his mind. He need not have concerned himself; the shrouding spell he had woven north of Great Blasket still held true. Somewhat self-consciously, he made an eldritch gesture and the golden skiff eased into the southern inlet. He raised his head and the fog-bank which had been idling off Slen Head cavorted into the bay, skidding at the turn towards Castlemaine before tumbling after him like an excited puppy at the anticipation of a walk.

As it caught him up, racing around and around as it licked at him affectionately, he found he had to calm the youthful entity with a stern, if silent, command. He could feel now the brooding presence of the prisoner on the belfry, the spell-muted terror of the animal in which it was confined, and see the wariness in the faces of the few sober inhabitants versed in the old ways as they watched the fog spill into their town. The latter always seemed to expect something or someone to burst from the broiling mass in some grandiose manner.

"More fool they," he whispered to the fog which shuddered with loyal mirth, at the same time being careful to smother, rather than carry, its master's voice as it escorted him to the deserted track Cathbad had selected. The Golden Torque rattled along behind him, somehow infusing a mixture of plaintive and disgusted tones into what would merely have represented normal clatter to the untrained ear. Cathbad waited until he was certain there was no-one about before transforming his robe into more contemporary wear, patiently describing what he wanted the fog to do before retracing his steps to lay hands on the recalcitrant Torque, pushing its grumbling bulk before him.

"This is unbearable," The Torque finally blurted, nearly succeeding in tripping the druid up with the rear wheel of its new form. Cathbad merely grinned, deftly avoiding the ill-tempered manoeuvre. "You're not really the last of the druids, you know," it added peevishly, hating the necessary transformation from skiff to bicycle. It shimmered slightly, noticing a picture on a page of a discarded catalogue ironed upon the hedgerow's border by a month's worth of concerted downpour.

"Nice," Cathbad noted admiringly of The Torque's improvement on his own basic notion of a bicycle; while the fog, following his instructions, condensed to form a crude rucksack. He added the finishing touches himself, sculpting the organic elemental to suit his needs. "There now, don't be frightened," he assured the startled fog in a soothing tone, "It won't be for long, just until I fix the spell imprisoning the fearsome one."

"Don't believe him," teased The Torque, "I've been like this for millennia."

"Sorcha," Cathbad reprimanded The Torque, "you're different, and you know it. If you hadn't been such a rebellious child and chosen to marry a mortal in a fit of pique, your children wouldn't have even dared think of defying Danu." He considered for a while, "besides, the fog doesn't know what millennia are."

153

"It wasn't just a fit of pique," Sorcha, or The Torque pouted, mischievously beaming images of the time of ice into the fog's consciousness.

"Now that's enough, and an exaggeration. Why can't you behave? It won't be long now. You don't want Danu extending the sentence, do you?" Sorcha was silent. No, she most certainly did not want Danu to consider such an option.

A car swept past them from the direction of Carrantuohill, only to screech to a halt three hundred yards down the road. A head like a seeding dandelion popped out of the driver's window, swivelled with the help of some unseen contortion and a chicken-wing elbow, and shouted back at them.

"Oh, it's yoursel," it called, trading in a suspicious frown for a welcoming smile.

"Tis," Cathbad returned, donning the brogue like an old cloak.

"You still up in the mixed city!" the old woman queried good-naturedly.

"No, it's here that I am," Sorcha quipped in Cathbad's voice, irritated at the jocular reference to Derry. The dandelion head bobbed appreciatively.

"That's a good'un. Is it ventriloquism you're studying now?"

"Shut up, Sorcha," Cathbad hissed beneath his breath. "No Mrs. Donaghy," he continued in a more conversational tone and volume as he pushed the bike down the road towards her, "but I've been performing at children's parties to keep bread on the table while I finish the novel." He hung his head as he closed on the car. "It's got so that it creeps up on me. Has a life of its own, so it does. I'm truly sorry for the snap."

"Snap?" she chuckled, waving him into the back seat of the four by four. "Sure I've known you years, and never once heard a hard word. I'd be a bitter oul biddy indeed not to take the humour as meant." She eyed The Torque appraisively. "You can throw that vain contraption on the rack," she said, patting a roof-frame obviously built for heavier fare than racing bikes, "and get in and rest yourself. I'm doin' no sailin' today an' I guess you'll be doin' little peddlin'." Her eyes twinkled. "You'd be here for the fair, of course. Is it a breeze through as usual, or would it you be of a mind to rest up

154

a mite longer after, for a change? The weather's fussy, and a weary traveller might stay at the house for a while. The daughter's back from U.C.D., you know, and has grown beautifully since you'ns last met."

Cathbad shared a bashful smile. Mrs. Donaghy was always on the match. Her daughter Roisin was indeed a beautiful girl with an infectious laugh, a generous soul, and dancing eyes; but Cathbad had ten thousand years on her and, to be truthful, was more than a little intimidated by her sensual energy. Besides, he told himself, he had a novel to finish. It wouldn't be fair to expect a young girl to hook up with a boring old fart with little income and a millstone of duties.

"You'd think ten thousand years and more would be enough time to amass a bloody fortune and get everything sorted out," Sorcha telepathically communicated from the roof as the car raced along the winding road. "It's expletive windy up here."

"*Expletive* windy?" he beamed back.

"Ever tried to swear, I mean really swear, telepathically? The intended word was, I assure you, not *expletive*."

"...was asking about you at Christmas break." Mrs. Donaghy was reporting, sharing her attention between shifting gear and the rear-view mirror. "Your rucksack's leaking."

Cathbad rebuked himself silently for losing concentration, and reinforced the spell containing the fog. He poked at the spillage with a finger, hastily pushing it back into shape.

"Just a piece of plastic sheet. Looks like liquid in this light," he lied.

"Oh, glad o' that. She's only new. Damn, now he has me at it. Why do men always regard machines as female?"

"I don't know," Cathbad dissembled, avoiding the traditional parallels of maintenance, contrariness, and expense. "Must be something about grace."

"Hah, you fraud. I know exactly why you do it. The question was purely rhetorical. Don't let the country or the crackle in the voice blind you to the craft in the head. Still, it was mannerly of you to lie." She executed a handbrake turn around a particularly vicious bend. "Always love doing that," she guffawed. "The oul boy won't have it when he's aboard. Sure you won't stay on?"

155

"I'd love to," Cathbad replied in all honesty, "but apart from probably not surviving the drive back to your place, my book's not for writing itself."

The old woman laughed heartily at his candour.

"Why don't you get one of those laptop thinggamies? You could write your book in between romancing." She gave a broad wink to the mirror. Cathbad could but grin.

"Sorry," he laughed, "I need to be totally isolated to write. No distractions."

"Ah, she'd be that all right," Mrs. Donaghy admitted. She was quiet until they passed the authorised campsite and reached the village. "How is it you can spare the time for the fair each year?" she posed accusingly, curiosity and frustration momentarily getting the better of her.

"Ah now," Cathbad touched the side of his nose, "that's a sacred duty, Mrs. Donaghy, not a pleasure; a solemn and secret obligation which I dare not neglect." The car slowed, stopped outside the post office cum grocers, and the little woman turned to face him with an incredulous eyebrow.

"Go'n away o' that ya rogue, you're here for your yearly piss up," she scoffed.

"Sure in't that a duty," Cathbad joked with a broad grin, climbing out of the vehicle. The would-be matchmaker donned a mock scowl, then relented.

"Roisin and me'll be at The Oak for lunch. Will you at least try an' join us?"

"Well," Cathbad prevaricated, retrieving The Torque form the hefty roof-rack, "I'd be delighted. Three? I've to be away for four to catch the eleven o'clock flight from Cork, and it's a long hard slog with no motor."

"Three it is. I'd give you a lift myself to the airport, but the cows and the big rooster indoors have to be fed and put to their beds, an' they'd never think to do it themselves." Then she was off with a wave.

"He's stronger this year. Have you the hurl and the stone rose?" Sorcha whispered as he pushed her towards the church.

"No, I thought I'd wrestle the Juggernaut instead this year for a bit of exercise. Of course I have them. I also have The Bones Of The Earth."

"You what? Where did you find them?"

"Shut up," he growled between clenched teeth as a reasonably sober reveller paused to stare, before shrugging and staggering further up the street. "I used the Horn Of Lug to conjure them," he internalised his response.

"That's not possible," Sorcha disputed, "they're protected from all magic."

"Only when in their original casket at the earth's magical core. Remember, they were stolen during the Druid Rebellion. Otherwise our friend up there could not have been summoned in the first place and of necessity chained to a lesser form."

"Yeah, yeah," snapped Sorcha. With a peculiar twist of thought she pushed a mental image of a hand tapping a watch into Cathbad's head, "haven't you got something to do other than give history lessons? Time's a wastin'." The druid restrained himself; she was, after all, quite correct. However… "Hey, HEY. Whatcha doin'? Where'd you get that chain?" Cathbad ignored her protests and calmly chained her to the church gates.

"Can't have my bike nicked, can I?" he returned sotto voce, smothering any further complaints with a containment spell. With a self-satisfied smirk, he turned his back on her and climbed the steps to the chapel doors, checked about for unwanted observers, then ducked around the side. Simultaneously reinstating the shrouding spell and releasing the fog from its enchantment, he allowed his faithful pet to carry him up the side of the building until he was floating about twenty feet away from this year's Puck.

Tied to the spire by a combination of rope and chain lest the animal either strangle, hang or dash itself on the flags below, the animal eyed him curiously for a moment; determinedly but unsuccessfully attempting to gain purchase on the rope with its teeth through the specially designed muzzle. Unexpectedly it lunged at him, only to be brought up short.

"Release me, druid, I need to fulfil my purpose," came the snarl, contorting the poor beast's mouth and features with the human words. The goat suddenly became fully and vividly aware of the inner presence, and thrashed about in terror.

"You know I can't do that, Baelin. You were summoned in anger by a mortal apprentice who was frustrated that he could never become a true druid. His hatred infuses you." Cathbad's voice carried compassion.

"Why torture me thus, then?" The eyes blazed red as they glanced over the parapet at the drunken humans even now gathering below for the annual spectacle; either pointing and laughing at the sight of a goat tied to a steeple, or bombarding the belfry with flash photography. "If I am not to be faulted, why this for so many centuries? Destroy me and be done."

"We may not destroy the children of Danu's sentinels, and we had not the power nor lore to safely free you, Juggernaut, until now." A flash of profound hope seeped into the shared eyes as, unseen to any below, save Sorcha, Cathbad whisked the hurl from nowhere, flicked the stone rose into the air and let it loose.

Rather than propelling the enchanted jewel into the body of the unfortunate goat to reinforce the annual spell of imprisonment, Cathbad altered his grip slightly, smashing the stone rose to smithereens, freeing the spirit of the Juggernaut and sending the goat into a forgetful sleep. Then, before the mighty entity could manifest its true form, or even react to its new-found freedom, Cathbad produced the Bones Of The Earth and bound Baelin's essence to them with a few arcane symbols drawn in the air between them. The druid could sense the heaving of the immense chest as he strove to break free. Cathbad took a deep breath.

"Rest now, child of Finn and Shannay. Be shackled no longer to mortal designs." Then he spoke the words. Like a mist, the presence melted, sighing as it was caught up by a passing breeze to dissipate into the evening sky, crossing the barrier and home.

Cathbad watched for a while, staring at the space even after the Juggernaut was gone; then returned to Sorcha. Wordlessly he lifted the containment spell, unchained her from the railings and wheeled her out of the square and Killorglin, to be cloaked and transported toward the southern inlet of the bay by fog and enchantment.

At the touch of sea-water Sorcha became The Torque once more, and bobbed up and down on the tide waiting for the druid to board. The fog swirled, impatient to be away, back to the open sea.

"Go on home," Cathbad urged them both.

"What?" Sorcha verbalised, heedless of who might be about.

"Go home."

"You need to get back to Derry, the oaks miss you." Sorcha objected. Cathbad sighed and shrugged.

"Derry will keep. I'll take the Monday flight," he grinned. "I have a different Oak to attend," he gazed out at the turbulent sea, "and it's high time I had a weekend off to attend to the mistletoe."

Which Way is Heaven?

by Natasha Monroe

She sees an angel fall off the edge of the world. Feet first, he drops into the deep blue sea, his small shouts lost on the wind, his little arms splashing, his head barely kept above water in imitation of an island.

She blinks, and he is gone again.

She watches him struggle underwater before coming up for air, God's fingertips pressed to his lips. *"Hush. Hush. Whisper who dares. Mammy is saying her prayers.´*

From the brink of a cliff she looks to the horizon, and says a prayer such as this: "Our Father. Who art in Heaven. I know where you live."

His address she will keep closed as a secret, like a page ripped from a bible. For there is, in this corner of the planet, a better sense of direction expected of a fisherman's widow with a drowned child.

The island was God's own country after all. It was the westernmost parish of Europe, the most westerly point of the nation, barely on the map. A fishing village, at the foot of a sacred mountain.

Up to now, Ellen had always had it, as every islander had it, and they were all related by blood, marriage, or both, that their ancestry stretched back no further than Noah. It was an undiscovered island until the Ark landed on the mountain peak, as God bade unto an Old Testament prophet: 'Rise and go to the western edge of the world: perchance the Flood may not reach it.'

"It's been pelting since," were her own words. Albeit the general consensus was God was only spilling holy water on their heads. Always He sent a rainbow after a downpour in reminder: never would he drown the world again. Or at least if He did – not them. Noah's ark-building hands guaranteed a Christian burial on dry land.

If the sea didn't get them first, that was. From Noah on, it was an island of boat-builders and fisherman. A place where death by drowning was routine, and bodies failed to turn up.

There being hardly such a thing as a fisherman, let alone a fisherman's son, who could swim - interference with Providence was a mortal sin – as soon as her relatives returned from the mainland fair, and heard Séan had yet to wash up, facedown, in a dead man´s lot, they would reach immediate unanimous agreement, "Your loss is God's gain." Obviously, to avoid ancient sinners gone out with the Flood, Séan was, like his father before him, by divine intervention, taken straight up to Heaven.

In his previous, mortal life, the same seven-year old bespoke a pagan's lines with pride. Up to this morning he believed what goes up must come down; we try to rise up, but fall into the Atlantic. Pretending to drown, we breathe underwater.
 ´The Gospel According To Séan´ he deemed valid as any biblical disciples: Noah was not the first man to land on the mountain peak, rather their ancestors were magicians. They had sprung from the ancient Celtic fairyrace of the Tuatha. A super-race, at once human and divine, who never knew death only immortality.
 Once upon a Flood, Séan surmised, to make way for the Ark, the Tuatha were blown off the mountaintop into the sea by a North-Atlantic gale of God's breath.
 Being immortal, Séan insisted, the Tuatha naturally *refused* to drown; instead, settled in an underwater kingdom they called Tír Na nÓg, a Land of Eternal Youth, and could to this day be seen riding fairyhorses upon the sea as if it were dry land – kidnapping drowned fishermen before God got there first - and whisking them to a submarine Paradise.

It was a story of heroes even God couldn't compete with. It was Séan's story and he stuck to it when he fell like Humpty Dumpty off a cliff.
 When the world ended again, Ellen waited for him to come home until the rain held its breath to let a rainbow out to play, and her six year-old nephew came dashing over the meadow, his cap, and her son, blown away.
 Doubled over, a stitch in his side, Liam stood at her garden gate, and stepped backwards from the truth. He gasped for oxygen, then took her breath away.

161

He pointed to the sea with magic in his eyes, "He went thataway!"

"Séan drownded himself," he yelled across the distance between them. "But he's not kilt at all."

He crossed his little heart, and hoped to die if he told a lie. "Séan got kidnapped. By the Tuatha. On the Holy Bible I'd nothing to do with it Aunty Ellen. God blew him off a cliff."

"Pray, pray, pray, aloud for your cousin's soul, Liam, alongside your own," she cried. "Loud enough so your poor mother can hear from the clouds, and your father from the pub."

Before she ushered Liam ahead of her to chapel, he explained when, where, how, why, once upon a time, there lived a little boy who died in the rain, and James already knew.

Liam didn't push Séan, Ellen understood, though he was going to. Before God got there first.

Before he got far as Heaven's gates, before God took him for Himself, Séan was playing on the forbidden territory of the cliffs.

It was his uncle James who took him to chapel that day with Liam. Afterwards, they were to go fishing en route to the mainland fair. On her return from earlier mass they crossed paths, briefly, on the doorstep – uncle getting his nephew to the church in time, winking, and "Can't be late for a date with God."

Over his shoulder, Séan carried a fishing rod bigger than him, to catch a fairyhorse with.

"But what if a fairyhorse catches *you?*" Liam whispered.

His voice grew serious as death. "You might have to have your funeral in the sea."

Automatically she made the sign of the cross. Then died of grief on her feet. As expected.

"Oh well," Séan sighed, "I'll just have to live forever in Tír Na nÓg then. But don't worry. I'll be back to haunt ye of course."

She bent to kiss his cheek, "Do you promise?"

"I promise." He swore it. Of course.

James joked, "You should have been drowned at birth."

They slipped through the gap of the door.

On the way, James met their cousin Thomas. The men dropped the boys outside chapel gates. Pointing them in the general direction of a back pew, they left to quench some almighty thirst that couldn't wait. They explained to a pair of angels: "It was God's will."

By nightfall, James would say over and again, "I warned the little devils to stay put."

His head will shake at an impossible velocity, spittle foam in the corners of his mouth. He'll think the wind whispers ´murderer´, and keep looking at his hands he'll call shovels that buried her son. "You'll never forgive me, will you?"

The gale force of her will knock him through a chapel door. Then help him up, fall into his arms, her tears mixed up with his. Whilst Liam shouts from the altar. "I asked God *and* my mother to find Séan. They never answered me."

James picked up a pint of holy water, her son picked up a deathwish. Séan went fishing for eternal life. He took no umbrella with him.

Long after the service ended, and everyone left for the fair, from chapel gates James still called to gather two prodigal sons in from somewhere faraway, in out of the rain. But by then it was too late.

By then, they had already travelled back in time, and made history repeat itself. They had already ventured into no man's land beyond the cemetery. They had already stepped over their ancestors´ dead bodies to cross the border of a fine line between life and sudden death.

Easily, they scaled a graveyard wall only adults could see over. On a windswept ledge, they stood, peering over a cliff into a hundred foot drop only God could survive.

They giggled and plotted in their Sunday best, delirious, wet. They carried prayer books, and imaginations mountain high, to play their favourite game. Holy War. And they were good at it.

In this game, Liam was God on a mountain top; Séan, the last magician left, laughing in the face of death, because he didn't know how to die, only live forever. He planned a mock kidnapping by the fairies.

He issued a breathless plea, before he left. Suicide he knew was a sin. So he called God down to earth, and asked Him a favour.

"Earth calling God. Come in God. It's me again. Séan O´Shea. World's End.

"I'm ready to get drowdned now," sobbed the waterproof wizard.

"I don't deserve to get to Heaven," he sniffed.

"Can you blow me off the cliff now please?"

Famous last words of a wizard, blown away in a powerful breeze - as promised.

Long seconds passed. Liam called out in boredom, "Are you immortal yet?"

"I'm not even kidnapped."

God counted, "One, two, skip a few... ninety-nine, a hundred," under his breath.

"Are you kidnapped NOW?"

Séan peered over at him in the deluge. (Still there. Of course. It was just a game.) No. He wasn't immortal again. Not yet.

For dramatic effect, he left Liam slipping in suspense. "No sign of the Tuatha yet but," Séan said.

Who could see salvation coming in blinding rain? But he had a plan B as well as a plan A. He boasted of stones in his pockets from a mountain field to sink him quick and deep. In the case of no pagan on a fairyhorse passing by, he would find submarine heaven himself.

Either way, he didn't question God's will when his cousin huffed and puffed his cheeks, and blew him away in the mostest powerful breeze ever. On earth.

He let it happen. Let the divine wind of his cousin's breath chase him to the brink.

He left before the game ended. In stitches at his own joke. Turning to bid a pretend farewell, on that blustery day, he lost his footing, slipped, in rainbow-coloured Wellingtons. Skidded on the precipice of a cliff. Dared too close to the edge of the world. The world ended.

Liam left out the parts unsuitable for fairytales. So did James; "Only the tide rushed to meet the magician."

James said Séan had already left by the time they came to claim him. The surf washed the crimson shape he must have made.

The rocks wiped his remains from their chests. The sky changed from grey to blue, drying the prayer book he left on a ledge. And the sea went about its business as usual.

Inch by inch they still searched a two by one mile island, knowing he must have flown over their heads.

But by nightfall he catches her leaning against a graveyard wall, crying in the chapel of her hands, in a game of Hide and Seek. Counting, "One, two, … this can't be true."

"It isn't."

She pricks her ears, hears footsteps too, swings north as a compass. Seawards.

She feels her heart change position. In her next breath, glow in the dark. She sees him standing there, right in front of her, in his sensible footwear. A boy who doesn't want to get his feet wet in a Flood.

A soggy angel. Telling fibs again. Hugging her hips, he looks up at her. "I fell out of the sky," he says. "I went to Heaven. Then I came back again. It rains in Heaven the mostest. That's why I'm all wet."

She blesses herself, bending to angel level. "Oh Séan you had me worried sick." Her anger melts to relief, love, and kisses, she holds him too tight. "You're squashing my invisible wings."

Somehow he wriggles free of her grip. "St. Patrick gave them to me. God wasn't there. He'd gone fishing."

For his next trick he vanishes, having practised wizardry before. Where angels fear to tread he reappears, in his former station, looking over his shoulder at her. "I have to hurry up. God's waiting in the ark."

Gathering her wits, she shoots up, arms outstretched, she takes baby steps towards him.

"Séan. Now Séan. Listen to me. You – you- you - you come back here this instant. You come back you hear? You come back to me… please. You come - back… to me… "

There is a moment, after she was about to jump, she stands under the new light of the moon, statue still. Feet planted on solid ground. As if

165

she wouldn't dream of moving. Head bowed, knees bent, hands in the prayer position. Awestruck eyes on the water.

Under a sky that lost its gravitational grip, so Heaven could move closer to earth, she spies the grand pageant of a horseman, more human than divine.

Triton-like, he rises. In an instant. Comes charging criss-cross the bay. The workings of pulled muscles traceable in motion, his stride is hit by what He is ordained to. His halo askew, he dives beneath the ocean's lid, reaches Séan with this lasso, says *"Hush. Hush. Whisper who dares,"* ropes him in. Catches a fish big as a child. Surfacing, her son yoked to his breast, the mast to his sail, he carries him away.

Her answered prayer, on a winter's night, He kidnaps an angel - before she gets there first.

Man, beast, and boy, as one, lean forward into the face of the wind, ears retreated, manes thrown back. They gallop past, across the waves, by some enchanted speed. Over a horizon of sea and sky, they ride, sure of their geography, and footing.

On an island on which rain misted the atmosphere, lending everything one saw the appearance of a mirage, they slip through a gap in the water, shattering the surface of things.

And the world moved swiftly along, deaf to the sound of some far-off explosion.

Having proved to Liam the sea holds nothing other than fish, James rows the boat ashore.

Holding hands, they look up, in unison, as she stares into that middle distance, pointing her finger at God. Give or take an inch, their gaze follows her directions. She permits them that standard eye witness account, when they can't find any missing angels on earth.

In perfect synchronicity, they fall to their knees, two saints, in the rain – eyes wide shut.

They take a God's eye view of the last look of Séan's life, in keeping with tradition. Through sheer blind faith, see him escape, another Jesus, over a graveyard wall. Rise up from a ledge against the laws of gravity, and myths. Fly sky high. Whole, holy, leaving wet footprints in his wake, walk right through Heaven's gates.

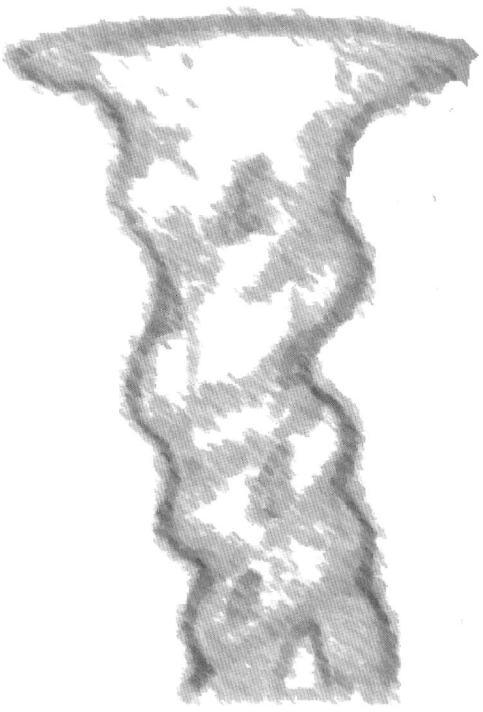

Kismet

the moon will not rise
the stars shine
the stars will not shine
the moon rises

the day will not come
the night goes
the night will not go
the day comes

the rain will not drop
the wind blows
the wind will not blow
the rain drops

the tree will not fall
the axe chops
the axe will not chop
the tree falls

the iron will not smelt
the fire burns
the fire will not burn
the iron smelts

the door will not open
it shuts
the door will not shut
it opens

Steve Mann